Edward Willett

Bob Brant, Patriot and Spy

A tale of the war in the west

Edward Willett

Bob Brant, Patriot and Spy
A tale of the war in the west

ISBN/EAN: 9783337297640

Printed in Europe, USA, Canada, Australia, Japan

Cover: Foto ©Andreas Hilbeck / pixelio.de

More available books at **www.hansebooks.com**

A TALE OF THE WAR IN THE WEST.

BOB BRANT,

BOB BRANT,

PATRIOT AND SPY.

CHAPTER I

Early Life of the Hero.

THE guns with which Beauregard opened fire upon Fort Sumter, made a great noise in the world, much greater, it is probable, than any of the artillerists who directed or worked them supposed they did or could make. They sounded in the remotest corners of the civilized world, and struck terror to the hearts of cotton operatives in Lancashire and Lyons, as surely as they inspired with patriotic indignation the loyal millions of the North. Their echoes resounded through every city, town, and village of the land, and caused a commotion and an excitement such as had never been known before, and such as few, if any, had expected.

To the call of the President for the seventy-five thousand men who were to march triumphantly through Secessia, and take, hold, and possess "the forts and other United States property" in that still unsubdued region, no people responded more readily and enthusiastically than the inhabitants of the small village of B——, in one of the counties of New York, bordering on the Hudson. Intense excitement prevailed among the young and the old, and a full company, which was all that could be accepted from the locality, was immediately raised, while some ardent and patriotic youths sought enlistments in regiments that were raised at a distance. Among the young men who were expected to be the most active in answering the call of the country, was Robert Brant, generally called Bob Brant, the son of a substantial farmer of that neighborhood. Young Brant had seen twenty-two summers, and probably just as many winters. He was a little above the medium hight, small limbed, but compact, his frame indi-cating great activity and endurance. He was neither handsome nor unhandsome, thus, being indifferently fitted for the hero of a love story; but in his broad forehead, keen gray eyes, compressed lips and solid chin, were written courage and penetration, with great firmness and determination. About the corners of his mouth lurked a love of the ludicrous, and good temper and strong affections were impressed upon his features. A calm, equable, and quiet nature was his, not easily excited, and seeming to grow cooler and calmer in the presence of danger, or of any emergency which called for the use of his highest faculties. In fact, he had never been taught in his boyhood, as too many children are, what to fear, and had not yet learned it. He was skilled in all athletic exercises, especially in swimming, having saved a companion from drowning, at the imminent peril of his own life, before he was out of his teens; and had made it a part of his education to bring his frame as near to perfection as he could. Take him all in all, Bob Brant was a strong man, in every sense of the term, and was loved, respected, or feared by those who knew him, according to their acquaintance with the man and appreciation of him.

The only son of his father—his mother being dead, Robert had enjoyed the advantage of an excellent education, and had made a tour over a considerable portion of the Union, which had added greatly to his worldly wisdom, in increasing his knowledge of men and things. Having graduated at a military school, his services were desired in the first regiment that was formed in his native county, and he was offered a Lieutenant's commission, which he refused, to the surprise of all his friends. He did not condescend to explain his refusal, simply saying to those who pressed his acceptance:

"When you come back, the war will begin."

The regiment went to the field, fully expecting to conquer a speedy peace, and returned at the expiration of their term of service, shortly after the close of the campaign which ended with the disastrous and humiliating spectacle of Bull Run. Its ranks were soon filled up for the three years' term, and Bob Brant was again urged to accept a commission, but again declined. It begun to be hinted that his loyalty was questionable, and one indiscreet soldier accused him of being either a traitor or a coward, but received a knock-down blow for his only reply, and thereafter, no one ventured openly to question either Bob Brant's courage or patriotism.

The regiment again went to the war, and Bob quietly continued his farming occupations, until the vast army which was thereafter to be known in history as the army of the Potomac was organized by General McClellan, and the hosts of the Union were ready at all points to meet the enemy.

One evening, on his return from the field, he told his father that it would be necessary to get a farm-hand in his place, as he was going away.

"Where are you going, Robert?"

"I am going to try to serve my country, and will not return alive while this war lasts."

· "But this is strange, my son," said the astonished Squire Brant. "You twice refused a commission in your own home regiment, and I do not see how you can better yourself elsewhere. Some of your neighbors have been free in calling you a secessionist, but I have had no fear of that. I hope, however that you don't intend to join the rebel army."

"There is not a drop of my blood, father, that is not true to my country, and you know it, so that it is useless to talk about that. I know a way in which I can be of more service than by accepting a commission, or enlisting in a regiment. If my old friends choose to call me a secessionist, it serves my purpose that they should do so. My path is not their path, and connection with them would not advance my plans. If they ever hear of me, they will have good cause to know that I am not a traitor."

"Are you fully determined upon this step, Robert, and do you feel that it is for the best?" said the squire, who placed entire confidence in the rectitude of intention and good judgment of his son.

"Fully determined, for I made up my mind to it long ago, and I know that it is the best I can do to serve the cause. I shall leave to-morrow, and will write you from Washington."

"Then go, my son, and may God go with you, and may the prayers of true patriots attend you. I shall feel that you are endeavoring to do your duty, and if you fall, I shall know that you die the death of a brave and honorable man."

Without more ado, Bob Brant packed up a few articles of apparel, took a good supply of money, bid farewell to his sorrowing father, and left the old homestead—perhaps forever.

His purpose he kept to himself, but it will soon appear.

CHAPTER II.

Brant in Washington.

To Washington Bob Brant quietly bent his course, not as one who gayly goes forth to seek his fortune or to meet adventures, but with a solemn purpose in his heart, from which no thoughts of danger or of death could turn him. He knew that his path was to be a rough one, and that he would owe much to his address or good fortune, if he escaped a painful and ignominious death. He also felt that in all probability he would get little thanks for his labor, and that the chances were in favor of poor pay, starvation, and a solitary death, far from friends or home. But of one thing he was assured, that he could serve his country in the course he had chosen, and serve it to some purpose. As he had said to his father, he was "fully determined," and consequences were not to be thought of.

If our hero could have been discouraged, he would have been driven back upon the threshold of his undertaking. As he was provided with a letter of introduction from the member of Congress of his district, he was civilly received at the Adjutant's office, but his intention was sneered at, and he was told that he could not be recognized in any capacity in the army; and that there was no provision for payment of the service in which he sought to engage; consequently, his fate must take care of itself, and his pocket also.

"I am glad to say that I am able to defray my own expenses," said Brant, "and as for my life, I expect to carry that in my hands. I only desire my name to be recorded in your office, so that I may refer to you, in case I should get in trouble among our own men, which might easily happen. I would also like a letter to some General, who would not object to my operating in his department."

"We have a corps of scouts here," said the officer, "and certainly do not wish to increase them; but we can give you credentials to the commander of any western post that you care to visit; and if you should get in trouble, and it should be convenient for you to refer to this office, we will be happy to testify to what we know of you."

Brant was satisfied, as it was useless to be otherwise. He felt the force of the proverb, "Blessed are they who expect nothing, for they shall not be disappointed." He took the letter that was given him, muttering, "small favors thankfully received," and prepared to leave for the West.

Before he got clear of the dusty and politician-infested city, Bob Brant had several opportunities of seeing the members of the "corps of scouts," with which, as he had been informed at the Adjutant's office, the army of the Potomac was so liberally supplied. There were lounging about the hotels and bar-rooms, a number of young men dressed in the Federal uniform, mostly attired as officers, who all seemed to have plenty of money, which they drunk, gambled, or billiarded away with a perfect looseness. This appeared to be the sum total of their occupation, if we may except a continual bragging of exploits which they had never performed, but which each was ready to swear to for the other. Some of them were attired in poor imitations of Confederate uniforms, and all seemed to take pleasure in publishing their business, as if there were no secrecy about the service. Occasionally one of them would absent himself for a while, and on his return would boast that he had made the round of the rebel camps, and profess to give accurate information of the numbers and designs of the enemy. But it is probable that they seldom went further South than Alexandria.

"None of that for me," said Bob, as he shook the dust of Washington from his feet, and took the cars for the West.

Following him, he next "turns up" at the semi-submarine "City" of Cairo, at the mouth of the Ohio, then rising into importance as the great military dépôt of the West, the point from which have been started the important expeditions which have prostrated the rebel power in Kentucky and Tennessee, and on a large portion of the Mississippi. He had presented his letters to General Grant, by whom he had been favorably received and kindly treated. General Grant was, (and still is, thank God!) a calm, quiet, silent man, of solid parts, strong common sense, clear judgment, great energy, and indomitable perseverance, entirely devoted to his profession. He was also, though no talker, an excellent judge of character, and was struck with the cool and determined nature of young Brant, which assimilated strongly with his own. The more the firm purpose and steady devotion of our hero became manifest to him, the more the General was pleased with him, and promised him all possible aid and protection.

"You are doubtless aware," said he, "of the principal points we must reach. The enemy has a strong force and extensive fortifications at Columbus, so strong, that a direct attack would involve a useless waste of life. Their principal rendezvous and camp is at Jackson, in Tennessee. At Fort Henry, on the Tennessee, and at Fort Donelson, on the Cumberland, they are strongly fortified, and probably have as many men as they think necessary for their defense. Of the strength of these garrisons, we can only judge from the contradictory accounts which reach us from different sources, and after all, it is little more than guess-work. We have scouts who pretend to have been there, and to be able to give us all the particulars; but I have no confidence in them. One of them gave evidence of having been in Columbus, by producing letters which he had stolen from the room of a rebel officer there; but, it is my opinion that he would sell one side as soon as another. It is important that we should know more than we do of these matters—but it is dangerous work, and death in such a service does not bring with it the glory that is found upon the battle-field. Still, I would not dissuade you from what I plainly perceive you consider your duty. There are many loyal men through western Kentucky and Tennessee, and a man who could go through there with his life in his hands would find many friends, if he could learn to know them."

"My course was taken a long time ago," replied Brant, "and I think no considerations of difficulty or danger can turn me from it. I thank you for your kindness and sympathy, and can only ask you to extend to me what facilities you conveniently can."

"You shall have all the protection that it is in my power to give," said the General; "but I fear that it will amount to little. I can say this, however; I know of at least ten rebel spies around our camps, men who claim to be citizens, and perhaps are, but who take every possible opportunity to send information to the enemy. They are well watched, and can do us little, if any harm; but I would be glad of a chance to make some of them feel the weight of the laws they are breaking. If the rebels should take you and maltreat you, at least one of these fellows will hang."

"Don't hang any one on my account, General, unless he ought to be hung. I will try hard to deserve death at their hands, before I meet it, and will get my satisfaction in advance."

"Don't be too confident, young man," said the General, as he thoughtfully chewed his cigar. "I suppose you will want some money—"

"No, thank you; I have sufficient for present purposes. If I come back, and should be 'short,' perhaps I may trespass on your kindness to cash a draft."

"You must be in earnest, my friend. Well, I must introduce you to Carson. But no—you will see him soon enough. Good morning, and don't be in a hurry to leave. You had better stay here a few days, I wish it. I will provide for your accommodation."

Brant had seen enough of the General to feel that his wish was equivalent to a command, and took his leave, saying that he would comply with his desire.

***

CHAPTER III.

Carson the Scout.

AFTER finding a lodging place, Brant walked around the levee and the town, to see what was to be seen. There was much bustle, but little excitement. In the camps, drills and parades were continually going on, and soldiers crowded the streets. At the levee, there were groups of citizens and soldiers, and a boat filled with troops had arrived. Others were lying at the bank, discharging ordnance and other stores.

Every thing betokened preparation, but preparation only, and the scene was a busy and interesting one.

It was hardly more than an hour after his interview with General Grant, that Bob Brant, as he was sauntering along the levee, felt a hand upon his shoulder, and a voice said quietly:

"You are my prisoner."

Turning around, Bob beheld a tall figure, dressed in black, but wearing a military cap, and with a cavalry sword buckled to his side.

"What's the matter?" said Bob, concealing his astonishment.

"Never mind—walk down to the guard-house, and perhaps you will find out."

"All right. Show the way, if you please, and let go my collar."

"I think I have you safe, when I hold your collar."

"I think I can walk alone," said Bob, wrenching himself free.

The tall figure again reached for his collar, when Bob astonished him by a blow between the eyes which made him reel. Bob thought if he had not had to reach so high, he would have "fetched" him.

As it was, the person he had struck gave him one fierce look, and beckoned to a couple of soldiers.

"Take hold of this man," said he, "and follow me to the guard-house."

As the odds were against him, Bob quietly succumbed, and marched along, closely held by a soldier on either side, followed by many curious eyes, as there had collected quite a crowd near the scene of the encounter.

His guide stopped at a hotel near the camp, and said roughly, turning to Brant:

"I suppose you will walk up to my room without troubling these men, or would you like to be carried up?"

Bob preferred to walk, and followed his captor up stairs. Entering a room, the latter locked the door, and said, as he handed his prisoner a chair:

"I hope you will excuse the rough way I have taken of making your acquaintance. Your name is Brant, I believe. Mine is Carson. You have heard of me from General Grant."

Robert intimated that he had heard of him, and took a calm survey of his companion.

"Carson, the scout," as he is known, and will be hereafter, in the history of the war, was a long, lean, and gaunt young man of twenty-eight or thirty years, with high cheek bones, black hair, and a piercing dark eye. He had entered the service in a cavalry company from Chicago, and when the company left for the East, he was persuaded to remain with the force at Cairo, where his intrepidity and address recommended him to the Generals commanding that post as a scout, in which capacity he continued, doing much and very essential service, until he met his death at the bloody battle of Fort Donelson, where his head was taken off by a cannon ball. He always went on his expeditions alone, and made many audacious excursions into Missouri and Kentucky, noting the locations of rebel camps and recruiting offices, and detecting the disloyal, at times bringing in two or three prisoners together, whom he had taken single-handed. He never knew what fear was, and his enterprise and ingenuity equalled his courage. It has been said that there was a dash of cruelty in his disposition, which he sometimes unduly displayed; but he was a brave man, and a noteworthy one. At all events, he is now a historic character.

"I must say," said Brant, "that it is rather a hard way to scrape an acquaintance, but I suppose you know what you are doing."

"Of course I do, and you will understand it when you know who and what you are. You are a secesh, from Indiana. Don't be surprised; there are lots of them there. You have friends down South, and you are trying to sneak through the rebel lines to get to them; and when you are down there, you want to make arrangements to ship over a lot of revolvers and gun caps. You see, I found all this out before you did. I shall almost think myself smart. The General likes you, and wants me to set you up in business, and this is the best way to do it. This arrest, and what will follow it, will get you an easy passage into Kentucky, if you play your cards well, and make you all right when you get there."

"I see a little light," replied Bob. "But, if I am a secesh from Indiana, what is my name?"

"Well, Errington—Henry Errington, that will do as well as any. Now, you must give me your parole—no, I can't take your parole, either—you can go about town under guard of one man, who won't trouble you much. I will hint around who you are, and what you are under arrest for, and you will soon find plenty of friends, who will ask you to drink as often as you want to. Do you ever drink, though?"

"Scarcely."

"Well, I want you to loaf around the bar-rooms, of which there are plenty here, and don't forget to edge into those that are kept on the sly. You will easily find sympathizing friends, and if they ask you to drink, you must take *something* occasionally, for that is the social style here and elsewhere. When you get a sure passage to Dixie, and letters to help you on your way, let me know."

Young Brant was then left free to go where he chose, and made the best use of his time in strolling around the levee and frequenting the drinking shops, accompanied by a soldier with fixed bayonet. The latter, however, took care not to be too near when any one entered into close conversation with his prisoner. The rowdy company and the reeking smell of the generally crowded bar-rooms were distasteful to the young man, but it was part of the business he had to do, and he went through it as he would have forded a river, or floundered through a swamp. He was quite an object of curiosity, and before the day was over had made several acquaintances, all inclined to be gay and festive, who sympathized with his supposed designs, and treated and pumped him more freely than was agreeable. He denied, however, any disloyal intention, though by his manner he contrived to leave his new friends certain of their man. At last, after a long conversation in a corner with a well-dressed man who unbosomed himself freely of his secesh sympathies, he felt himself touched on the shoulder as he came out, and on looking around, met the bright eyes of the inevitable Carson.

"That's your man," said the scout.

Robert took the hint, and improved his acquaintance at the next meeting, and carried out his assumed character of a secesh sympathizer wishing to go South. The result was, that his new friend went to headquarters, and certified to his loyalty, saying that he had known him well in Indiana. Robert was set free, and his friend was permitted to suppose that his certificate had effected his release. The next day, the young man received letters to parties in Jackson, Grand Junction, Memphis, and Tennessee, introducing him under the name of Henry Errington, and recommending him to the favorable consideration of the secesh generally.

Going up the railroad a short distance, he struck across the country, in company with his new-found friend, to the Ohio River, which he crossed at Paducah, where he easily got within the rebel lines.

CHAPTER IV.

Bob Brant's interview with Major Mercer.

JACKSON, Tennessee, is, or was before the war, one of the most pleasant villages in the State. Next to Memphis, it was the abode of the wealth and fashion of Western Tennessee, and was distinguished by many fine residences, surrounded by beautiful gardens and grounds. The inhabitants were generally wealthy, and possessed of a fair degree of intelligence and refinement. They were strong and "original" secessionists, and the disunion feeling was increased by the presence of a large rebel force in the town. It was one of the principal military rendezvous of the rebel forces in Western Tennessee, their chief camps of instruction being here and at Grand Junction. The post was under the command of General Cheatham, of Tennessee, and the force was variable in numbers, recruits continually arriving, and trained regiments being as constantly sent off. Jackson is changed now, and its people have reaped a portion of the reward of their treason. Most of them are self-exiled from their homes, and those pleasant homes have felt the devastating touch of war, and are pleasant no longer.

Nearly a mile from the town, a little back from the road, stood the mansion of Major Mercer, a plain, large, and roomy house, surrounded by tall trees and well-cultivated grounds, with a number of log buildings, for negro quarters and other purposes. Major Mercer was a gentleman of wealth and education, well known and respected in that region, having filled several important offices under the State. He had not been an "original" secessionist, but had, for some time, quietly used his influence in favor of the Union. Times change, however, and men change with them. Major Mercer, after a while, permitted considerations of policy and prudence to dictate his course, and fell into the secession current. It was an unwilling submission, made against the impulses of his heart and the

warnings of his better judgment; but it seemed better to him than the prosecution and banishment which has been the fate of so many. Spite of his change of course, Major Mercer was soon made aware that he was an object of suspicion to his neighbors, and to the Confederate authorities, and was continually subjected to annoyances which did not tend to increase his love for the new state of things. He chafed in the harness, and the hateful surveillance of the military commanders and the despotic government of the Southern oligarchy became daily more insupportable to him. On several occasions he had almost resolved to throw off the slack allegiance which he held to the "Confederate States of America," but the thought of his family and his property restrained him. The Major was a hale and hearty man of about sixty years of age, greatly loved and respected by his family, which consisted of his wife, his son, Charles, his daughter, Mabel, and twenty or more negroes of all ages.

Mrs. Mercer was a fine, matronly lady, entirely devoted to her family, and worthy to be the mother of such a girl as Mabel. Mabel Mercer had reached "sweet seventeen," and was a tall and spirited dark-eyed beauty, of the style that comes to maturity so soon in the South. She was healthy, active, and full of life and animation, the darling of her parents, and greatly beloved by the negroes of the place. Charles was about nineteen, tall, straight and handsome, and prided himself upon his riding and shooting accomplishments.

It was nearly dusk when our friend, Bob Brant, mounted upon a nag with which he had been supplied by one of his secesh friends in Kentucky, drew rein at the door of Major Mercer's mansion, and, throwing his bridle to a grinning darkey, asked for the Major.

Being ushered into the parlor, he was received in a gentlemanly, but cool manner, by Major Mercer, who had grown to be distrustful of all strangers. Bob merely handed him a letter, which was a note of introduction which he had got at Paducah. The Major perused it carefully, but with a displeased countenance, occasionally glancing at the bearer of the letter, as one would eye a snake or a toad.

"Well, sir," he said, at last, "I may as well tell you, plainly, that there is no use in bringing such letters to me. You have come to the wrong shop to sell your sneaking treason. If I ever supported this secession swindle, and I am ashamed to say that I have, to some extent, I am sick of it now, and I care little who knows it. I understand you are a Northerner, Mr. Errington."

"Yes, sir; from Indiana."

"Then, sir, I will give you my opinion of you, and if it will do you any good, you are welcome to it. Our Southerners, traitorous and mean though they are, have at least some excuse for their attempt to subvert the only decent government ever established on earth; but you, sneaking, despicable men of the North, who uphold them in their course, and aid and abet them, whether you do it from motives of gain or from any other motive—you certainly can't have any better one—are—well, no words can measure my contempt for you. There, sir, you can report my words to General Cheatham, or any one else, as soon as you choose. A man who would go into such an abominable business as you are engaged in, is just mean enough to do so."

The Major's face was almost purple, and his manner expressed that he meant every word he said. Bob began to feel himself in an awkward position, especially as a very well defined sneer of contempt curled the lip of the fair Mabel, and there was a twitching motion about the toe of Charley Mercer's boot, as if that young gentleman was itching to try his kicking abilities on the intruder.

It was awkward enough, but Brant speedily formed his resolution. Calmly opening his penknife, he slit the lining of his vest, and extracted from it a small folded paper, which he handed to the Major.

"If I can't sell my treason here, perhaps you would like to look at something of this kind."

Major Mercer glanced over the paper, and read as follows:

"HEADQUARTERS, DEP'T. OF CAIRO, }
"Sept. 9th, 1861.   }

"Pass the bearer, Robert Brant, in and out of the lines at his pleasure, until further orders, on service of this command.
"U. S. GRANT, Com'dg."

The expression of the Major's countenance changed instantly from anger to astonishment. He eyed his visitor more kindly, but still suspiciously.

"I don't understand this, sir. What does it mean? Who and what are you?"

Bob answered him boldly, and almost defiantly. He was by no means sure of the ground he stood on, but thought it best to dash right through, trusting to his audacity and ingenuity to bring him out safely.

"It means simply this—that I am in the secret service of the United States, and expect to stay in it as long as life is left me, and this rebellion lasts. My name is Robert Brant, and I have less sympathy with rebels than with horse-thieves; and all the pistols they will get from me may be put in the corner of Jeff Davis' eye, without interfering with his vision. Now, sir, I have told you the truth; my life is in your hands, and, as you just remarked, you can report my words to General Cheatham, or any one else, as soon as you choose."

Bob Brant was bold in making this declaration. In fact he was rash, and he felt the imprudence and danger of his course. His rashness can only be accounted for by the bright eyes of Mabel Mercer, which affected him strangely, and made him think there was something worth loving, besides his country and his flag. He felt as if he would rather be hung, than that she should regard him as other than a true man.

He was rewarded, for the bright eyes beamed kindly and sympathetically upon him, and the sneer which had curled Mabel's lip gave place to a smile.

Charley Mercer's boot stopped tapping the floor. He did not seem desirous of kicking any one.

The Major sat down and said nothing. He still seemed unsatisfied, and uncertain whether to welcome his guest or dismiss him. The matter was settled by the soft voice of his wife.

"I think, Mr. Mercer," said she, "that the young gentleman had better stay with us to-night. For my part, I am prepared to trust him, and, since he has reposed so dangerous a confidence in us, I think we can do no less than be equally generous with him."

The smile that then lit up Mabel's face was certainly one of assent, and Charley Mercer broke in with:

"As far as I am concerned, I am willing to bet on him."

Bob Brant felt better, but still retained his bold and defiant look, except when he glanced at Mabel, in whose countenance he saw an interest and a sympathy which he was glad to have excited. He felt that if he should not be able to sell his imaginary pistols, he would have no trouble in disposing of a heart.

CHAPTER V.

The Scout at Major Mercer's.

So the matter was settled, for Major Mercer, although still unsatisfied, was accustomed to rely much upon the impulses, as well as the judgment of his wife.

Mrs. Mercer rung a bell, and instantly entered a stalwart darkey, bright-eyed and grinning, the suddenness of whose appearance might easily induce the belief that he had been listening at the door. Mrs. Mercer was plainly of this opinion.

" Pharaoh," said she, " have you been listening to what we have been saying ?"

" No, Miss Car'line, I'd jes' come up the starway, an' was gwine on up when the bell rung."

" Well, tell Jim to take care of this gentleman's horse, and you take his carpet-bag up to the north room, and have Betse see that the room is in order."

" Oh, yes, Miss Car'line, I'll tell Jim, and I'll take the baggage up stars, right away, I's glad to take *his* baggage, I tell you," said the negro, grinning from ear to ear, and looking wondrously sly.

" What do you mean, Pharaoh ? Don't stand there like a laughing hyena, but tell me, instantly."

" Oh, Miss Car'line and Massa Harry, that young gen'leman won't hurt ye. He's one of the right sort. He's all right on the goose."

" Why, you black scoundrel, what do *you* know about the young gentleman ?" thundered Major Mercer, rising from his seat. Bob was also surprised, for he could not remember that he had ever seen the sooty features of Pharaoh.

" Oh, Massa Harry—now, Massa Harry— don't you go to put yourself in a passion, I ain't done no harm. But I seen that young gen'leman afore, Massa Harry, and I know he's one of the right sort."

" Pharaoh, what does this mean ?" said the perplexed Major. " Where have you seen him, and when ?"

" Now, Massa Harry, don't you go to put yourself in a passion, I ain't done no harm. I know you and Miss Car'line ain't none of them sheceshers, and you don't like 'em, no more'n they don't like you, and I ain't done no harm. But you know, Massa Harry, when you sent me 'way up to Massa William's to help him with his tobacca ?"

" Yes, what of it ?"

" Well, Massa Harry, I done didn't go thar at all, but struck across the woods and the canebrakes, and made a straight chute for Cairo, and there I saw all the sogers, and the splendid officers, an' the forts, an' the big guns, and lots of folks, and I saw *him*, too," said Pharaoh, pointing at Bob Brant.

" What did you see of me ?" said Bob, who was as much astonished as Major Mercer himself.

" Guess I seen you when Massa Carson put his paws on you, and you hit him that clip in the face. Hi ! Massa Carson mighty sharp feller, if he do look ugly an' hungry. He tole me you war comin' down here, an' he tole me to look after you, an' help you if I could. You seen ole Bill Woodworth yet ?"

" Old Bill Woodworth !" said our hero. " No, I don't know any such man."

" Well, ole Bill knows you, and he'll see you 'fore long. He's one of dem scoutchers, too, but he don't dast come 'round here— they know him too well."

As Major Mercer still stood astonished, not knowing what to say, Pharaoh went on eagerly to make a further explanation :

" You see, Massa Harry, I tole them officers, the Adjuram-Gen'l an' the rest, that we wasn't all sheceshers down here, and that our folks wasn't sheceshers at all, though we didn't know how long we could hole out; and they tole me we must jest hole out any how, and Massa Linkum's army would be down here, 'fore long ; and they axed me, wouldn't I like to stay up there an' be free, an' I tole 'em I wasn't gwine to leave the old woman an' the chilluns, an' wasn't gwine to leave Massa Harry an' our folks neither. And Massa Carson tole me to come right straight down here, an' he showed me that young gen'leman, and says, if I see him down here, I must 'member he's an awful shecesher, an' he mind him eye, and I know how big a shecesher *he* is. Hi !"

" That will do, Pharaoh," said Major Mercer. " Now take the carpet-bag up stairs, and have the horse attended to, and mind you keep your mouth shut before the rest of the servants."

" And, Pharaoh," said his mistress, " no more of your listening at key-holes in this house."

" Oh, Miss Car'line !" ejaculated the grinning African, as he skedaddled with Bob Brant's small amount of baggage.

Major Mercer gave a sigh of relief as he

resumed his seat, and his countenance looked much brighter than it had during the evening. Reaching out his hand to our hero, he said:

"You will pardon me, Mr. Brant, or rather Mr. Errington, as we must call you here, for my suspicions. But our circumstances compel us to be distrustful of strangers, and you must admit that you came in a very questionable guise."

"Of course, Major Mercer, I fully understand your situation, and you do not owe me any apology. Allow me to say that the revelations of your man, Pharaoh, have surprised me. I have no doubt that he has told you the truth, for the Carson he speaks of, is a scout in the Union service, and he made a sham arrest of me, in order to give me the character described in the letter of introduction which I presented to you."

"It has let in a new light upon me," answered the Major. "I feel now, as I have not felt for a long time, that the world is not made up of traitors, and that we have a country yet, with the power and the will to save us from secession despotism. But this is a dangerous trade you have taken up, sir, and I hope," he continued, his fears for his family and his property inducing a return of his timidity, "that your presence here may not endanger the safety of my family; for I must temporize, sir, I must temporize."

Bob blushed, not for himself, but for Major Mercer's manhood, and an indignant flush spread over the cheeks of Mrs. Mercer and Mabel.

"As for the danger to myself," said our hero, "I have found, so far, that the peril is less than I had supposed it to be, and see no reason to fear for myself. As for compromising you, I can assure you, that if I am found out by the enemy, it will not be here; and I am certain, that so far from endangering your safety, the chances are that I will be able to render you some service. I am not at all rash or careless, although my disclosure of myself to you might cause you to think so; but I was induced to do that by an impulse which I felt must be right, and I did not wish to appear to your — family — Bob's eye was on Mabel as he spoke—in the light of a sneaking Northern traitor."

"Pardon me again," said the Major. "Pardon me. I love my family so deeply, and fear for them so much, that the thought of them sometimes makes me a coward, as it has almost made me a traitor. Wife and son, draw up your chairs, and you too, Mabel. We must be careful how we talk, even among ourselves, for some ears might be listening which are not as honest as those of old Pharaoh."

The family then drew closely together, and discussed the present and the future in an anxious but quiet tone. Whether by accident or design, Mabel Mercer sat very near to Bob Brant, and as he heard her soft and musical voice chime in the conversation, like sweet bells sounding afar off, and at times caught the rich odor of her warm breath, he was lifted into an elysium, and his brain whirled until he found it difficult to fix his mind upon the matter in hand. He felt as if he would like to spy into her heart, and organize himself into a foraging party to capture her love, and then confiscate her in the name of the Union—not the "old" Union, but the kind of Union that a minister is needed to consummate. If General Grant could have known his feelings then, he might have distrusted the discretion of his young scout.

They talked long and earnestly; Bob urged upon Major Mercer the policy of moving up into a free State, if he could get away, taking a farm and hiring his negroes on it, if he could get them away. Of course the young man could not have been thinking of Mabel, when he made this very sensible proposition. The Major was puzzled about his negroes and his other property. Brant said that the negroes, in any event, would have to follow the fortune of war, and if the family staid at Jackson, it was probable that the rebels would drive them further South, and if not, the progress of the Union armies would force them. If the Major wished to promote their welfare, and had confidence in them, it would be better to keep them near the North, as they would never be of any use to him if taken further South. The Major recognized the justness of these remarks, but was still perplexed, and even spoke of the high prices he could get for them down below.

This was too much for Mabel and her mother, who scouted the idea of selling any of their servants.

"I had rather see them all free," said the matron, forcibly.

"Sell them for what?" said Mabel, "for Confederate money? Don't let your fears for us run away with you, father."

The matter was settled at last, as matters

generally were, by the clear sense of Mrs. Mercer, who proposed that they should move, as soon as they could, to her brother's farm, in —— County, Kentucky, as he had land enough and to spare, with a good house that was empty. After the many objections of the Major had been overruled, this plan was generally agreed to, and as the conversation had reached late into the night, the family dispersed to bed, with lighter hearts than they had known for a long time.

As Bob Brant laid down, his head and heart were full of Mabel Mercer, to the exclusion of everything else, and it was some time before his excited thoughts would suffer him to stop.

CHAPTER VI.

Divided Duty of Bob Brant.

Our hero was astonished, on waking from his sound but not dreamless sleep, to see the sun shining through his window. He was also saluted by a mocking-bird in a cage not far off, (in Mabel's room, as he thought,) which seemed to have learned a new tune. It said, as his half-wakened senses translated it:

"Bob Brant's—a humbug. Bob Brant's—a humbug."

And it struck Bob that he *was* a humbug. He asked himself severely, if that was any way to attend to the business to which he had devoted his life, to fall in love at the start (as he could not help confessing that he had) with a girl he had never seen before, and to permit her image to occupy his mind and heart, to the damage, if not destruction of the serious affairs he had undertaken. His life was too dangerous, he said to himself, to ask her to share it, even if she could be induced to do so. On the spur of the moment, Bob Brant formed several very excellent resolutions, of which, not the easiest was, that he would thereafter shut out all thoughts of Mabel Mercer. He dressed himself and went down stairs, looking savagely solemn.

As he stepped out into the garden, he heard the musical voice of Mabel Mercer, singing to herself, and caught a glimpse of her airy form as she moved about among the flowers. Unconsciously, as he persuaded himself to believe, he went toward her, and soon stood by her side, when she greeted him with a smile which made his heart throb violently, and played the mischief with his severe and excellent resolutions.

"Good morning, Mr. Brant—Errington, I mean."

"Good morning, Miss Mercer, and please don't let your tongue trip so any more, as it might possibly prove a death warrant for me, though it would sound sweetly, and could be met cheerfully, if it came from your fair lips."

"Oh, you are complimentary. Is that the way with you gentlemen of the North? Well, I don't like compliments, and am sure that nothing could induce me to speak your death warrant—or the death warrant of any other good Union man," she continued, half blushing. "If you could say, Mr. Errington, that I am a true Union girl, who would be willing to suffer and die for my country, it would be a compliment that I would be glad to hear."

"Indeed, Miss Mercer, I believe that I can say it, and I thank God that it is so. I only wish there were more like you—though there could be none like you," he said, musingly.

"No, there are few, if any, Union ladies around here," said Mabel, refusing to understand the compliment. "Don't you think, to change the conversation, that you are now engaged in a very perilous business?"

"Perilous it may be, and I expect it will be; but long ago I solemnly devoted my life to it, and I can afford to die better than many who must leave behind them pleasant homes and sweet family ties."

"Have you no one, then, to mourn for you, if you should fall in battle, or meet a more ignominious death?" said Mabel, shuddering.

"None, Miss Mercer, except my old father, who does not expect to see me return."

"Is there no fair lady who would grieve when you are gone?"

"None."

"Would it not make your heart better for your work, and please and comfort you, to know that some one, however insignificant, cared for you, and would mourn your loss, if you were to die?"

"Indeed it would," said Bob Brant, lifting up his flushed and then handsome face to the dark eyes that seemed to look into his soul.

"Then I assure you that *I* would grieve for you—oh, so much! for you are a true

Union man, and a brave one," she said, blushing deeply, " and such deserve my best prayers and sympathies. If this can ever comfort you, and keep you from risking your life unnecessarily, I shall be very thankful," and Mabel Mercer gave him her hand, smiling, blushing, and half weeping.

It was too much. As Bob Brant felt the warm and tender pressure of that small hand, his very fine resolutions melted, and the capture of the scout was completed. He had found something besides his country to love, and felt, but did not deplore, the " divided duty."

The breakfast bell soon rung, and Bob and Mabel Mercer went to the house. It may be said, in justice to our hero, whose performances and vascillations of late may cause him to be considered by some as not a "first-chop" hero, that he had enough good sense left to eat a substantial breakfast, and well he might, it being a good one.

After breakfast he started out to attend to " business." He declined the company of Charley Mercer, who was anxious to go with him, fearing that he might bring the young man into difficulty.

" I had better see for myself how the land lays," said he. " If I should possibly come to grief, I would not wish it to be known that I had any thing to do with this house or its inmates. If I should not succeed perfectly, you must not look for me here again. And so good-by, as we may not meet again."

Bob's whole heart was in his eyes when he looked at Mabel, and pressed her hand at parting, for he felt that it *might* be an eternal good-by.

But down the road he walked, gayly and almost joyfully. If he had been a musical hero, our hero would have sung or whistled as he walked, but as he was a very matter-of-fact sort of an individual, and had no ear for music, he did nothing of the kind. Before, it had been a determined and patriotic, but solemn and severe spirit that actuated him; but now he felt cheerful and lightsome, and better able to do and to dare, as well as to suffer. If it was Mabel Mercer who had wrought this change in Bob Brant, blessings on her sweet face !

Bob found his "business" better, and more easy of accomplishment, than he had expected. Delivering a letter to a prominent secessionist, who proved to be a " sure-enough" one this time, he was warmly welcomed, and introduced to several army contractors and officers, including General Cheatham himself. He had reason to thank the timely foresight of Carson, who had arrested him at Cairo, and thus given him a ready passport to Secessia, for the story of his arrest had preceded him—such was, at that time, the facility of communication between Cairo and the Confederate camps—and he found himself quite a lion.

He was astonished at the discipline and organization of the troops he saw at Jackson ; it was so different from what was reported and generally believed at Cairo. The men, also, were substantially, though roughly clothed, and seemed to be well fed. Bob wished that the same spirit of energy and activity that characterized the Confederate officers might be manifested by those on our side. It seemed to him that they appeared to feel that they had a powerful enemy to encounter, while the Union men were too confident, and too ready to underrate their adversary.

Bob made contracts with several parties for such a quantity of "navy-sized revolvers" as he thought would be reasonable, deliverable at any point within the Confederate lines at which he could most conveniently run the blockade ; also for gold lace and such other small articles as he could smuggle through. To carry out his idea of " business," he was careful to chaffer about the price, enlarging upon the increasing difficulty of getting his goods across the river, and endeavoring to get as much of the price as possible payable in gold. In short, he was entirely successful, being welcomed as a " friend in need," and made such good use of his eyes and ears, that before evening he had secured considerable information that would be very valuable in Cairo.

After sauntering about as much as he chose, he slipped away from his new friends before any of them had time to ask him home to supper, and took the road to Major Mercer's.

CHAPTER VII.

Threatening Appearances.

As Bob Brant sauntered along the road, he felt the perplexities of his situation, and, in plain language, was considerably bothered.

He knew that the information he had gained should be conveyed to Cairo, and that, too, with the greatest possible dispatch, and he knew of no way of getting it there but to carry it. He felt that a sudden disappearance from Jackson would cause him to be looked upon with suspicion by the Confederate authorities, and he feared that the suspicion might also attach to Major Mercer and his family. Can it be possible that Mabel Mercer had any thing to do with his perplexity, and that his desire of remaining near her for a short time caused him to hesitate? It hardly seems possible that any thing could cause a young man, who had formed such excellent resolutions, to deviate from his duty.

Nevertheless, Bob Brant was perplexed, and walked along in a kind of brown study, noticing nothing by the way, until he suddenly found himself surrounded by a rough crowd, who all seemed to have been drinking very freely, for they came on whooping and shouting, and were certainly intoxicated with excitement or poor whisky.

The spokesman of this interesting assemblage was a tall, raw-boned, gaunt individual, dressed in a rough suit of brown homespun, who flourished a heavy overseer's whip, and appeared as much overcome by intoxication or excitement as any of the rest. He had a merry twinkle in his eye, however, and his general appearance was indicative of mischief rather than malevolence.

This worthy staggered up to our hero, and shouted, as he brandished his whip in the air:

"Here, boys; shouldn't wonder if we have caught one of them durned Yanks at last. Let's look into the crittur."

Then sidling up to Bob Brant, who kept his right hand in the pocket where his pistol was concealed, with a maudlin air, said:

"Hello, stranger; p'raps ye can jest tell us whar ye come from. Seems kind o' strange for a man of your stamp to be found around here, 'specially with all them good clothes on, and nary Confederate uniform. P'raps ye'd jest let me know, for the satisfaction of myself an' this yere party of royal—loyal, I mean, boys—hic—citizens, who ye are, and whar ye come from, and all about ye. That's it, boys, and that'll bring this feller down to the pint of a toadsticker."

"That's the idea, ole fel," said one of the party, who was steadying himself up against a tree; "bring him down to tell which he came from, and whence he's agoin' to.

That's the question. Young feller, answer that ere speech."

Bob kept his presence of mind, and kept his hand on his pistol, both, as he thought, very needful things to be kept. And he answered them coolly and well:

"If you want to' know where I came from, gentlemen, I must say that I came from the North, from the State of Indiana. I am here to aid the Confederate Government by supplying them with arms and accouterments. I have some of the arms with me, and this is one of them," said he, drawing his pistol, cocking it, and presenting it at the crowd.

"There, never mind," said the individual who was steadying himself against the tree. "I s'pect it's all right, Cap'n, and I don't reckon he'd steal any niggers."

"No, it ain't, by a durned sight," said the long personage with the overseer's whip. "I've seen too much of these Indianny and Ellinoy Yankees, who come down here to swindle us, and go back and tell all they know. Say, stranger, tell us whar yer goin' to now. Ye needn't handle yer six-shooter, for we're too many for yer. So tell us plain and squar, if you've got any plainness and squarness about yer."

"I have only one thing more to say to you," said Bob, as he returned his pistol to his pocket, but left it cocked, and still clutched it firmly; "if you want to know any thing more about me, just go to headquarters, and ask General Cheatham about Mr. Errington. I have periled my life for your Confederacy, and don't mean to be insulted by any understrappers."

It was evident that the cool and deliberate Bob Brant was getting excited.

"It's all right, Cap'n, I guess," said the man who was steadying himself against the tree, and who had been gradually edging himself out of the possible range of Bob's pistol.

"No, it ain't all right, by a durned sight, as I told ye before," said the long and ugly one, who had stayed close to Bob during the parley. "I ain't satisfied with everybody's say-so, and I've good reason not to be, and I'm going to arrest this yere young feller, in the name of the Southern Confederacy."

Bob's hand again clutched his pistol, and his interrogator saw the movement.

"Ye needn't handle yer pistol, young man, for I'm able to take yer by myself alone, and can shoot a durned sight quicker than you ever dar'd to. Here, you fellers, go up the street, and turn off on that lane to your right, and see if you can pick up any more stragglers. And the first whisky-shop you come to, take a drink at my expense, and tell 'em Captain Higley will see it settled for. I'm goin' to take this yere young chap to the Captain's quarters, and ye can bet yer bayonets that the old man will fix him."

"All right, Cap'n," said the self-constituted synod, as they took their devious way along the road.

"Come along, young feller," said Bob's captor, as he staggered up alongside of his prisoner.

Bob concluded to go. He thought he saw plain sailing before him, and it seemed an easy matter to get rid of the inconvenient presence of this inebriated individual at any moment.

So they went along together, the tall man walking on the right of our hero, who stepped freely but warily, his hand still grasping his pistol. In a few minutes they came to a tavern in the road, where thick woods spread upon either side, and here Bob's conductor cast a quick and furtive look behind, and then suddenly staightening himself up, stopped in his tracks, and looked at Bob.

Bob Brant stopped also, and again clutched his pistol as he looked the supposed Confederate full in the face.

"Mr. Brant," said the long man, from whom every trace of intoxication had disappeared in an instant; "'spect likely ye don't know me."

"No," said Bob, "I don't."

"But I know you, and ye'll know me, when ye hear my name. Wouldn't those chaps hev give a pretty sum to know it, though! But it takes old Bill Woodworth to fool 'em!"

"What!" said Bob Brant, "do you mean to say that you are old Bill Woodworth? Here, where a price is set on your head! How can you dare—"

"Never mind, young man, what I dare. So ye thort I was a Confed, and drunk at that! Well, I meant ye should, but if any man has got good cause to hate the Confederates an' whisky, too, it is me. Between them, they've ruined my house and home, an' murdered my wife and child. I'll remember Missouri for 'em, and get revenge enough before I die. Do you know I went on tick for them fellers whisky? P'raps Captain Higley or somebody else 'll come

along and pay for it. Cuss 'em! I only want a clear field and a good rifle to show 'em what I think of 'em. But I hevn't no time to talk, or to cry, neither, though God knows I would like to. Carson sent me to meet you, and the Gineral said you'd hev some drawin's or writin's to send up. If you have, give 'em to me quick."

Bob had been astonished for a moment, at the audacity of this man, who was known and "spotted" by the Confederate authorities in all that section of country; but recovering his presence of mind, he drew from his pocket a few condensed notes and memoranda, and a small plan of the fortifications at Columbus, and handed them to his strange companion, who immediately thrust them in the breast-pocket of his butternut coat. The plan was complete, and the memoranda were of the utmost importance.

"Good-by," said Woodworth, hurriedly, wringing the hand of our hero. "The old man wants you to be in Fort Donelson within four days, ef you dar to do it."

"Dare!" said Bob, flushing up, "I will be there within the time, if I die for it."

"Yes, yes, that's what he said he knowed of yer. Git in as well as you ken; I can't tell you nothin' about it; but I'm 'feard the biggest trouble will be to git out. Let me tell you one thing—jest you take the Maysville road when you go. Good God! I'm off. Say you don't know me, young man," and in an instant, the long, gaunt, and ugly individual disappeared in the woods.

Bob Brant was somewhat surprised; as may reasonably be supposed, but his surprise was at an end when half a dozen Confederate cavalrymen, headed by a Lieutenant, rode up and halted where he stood.

"Halt!" said the officer. "Two of you guard this man, while the rest chase that fellow up. Catch him or kill him!"

The four disappeared in the wood, and two dismounted and took hold of our hero, to whom the almost breathless Lieutenant thus addressed himself:

"Well, sir, you are caught, are you? A pretty piece of business this is, and you shall swing for it, as sure as I hate a sneaking Northern spy. You have done for yourself this time, young man."

"I have done nothing wrong that I know of," said Bob, quite coolly, "and will be much obliged to you if you will tell me what this all means."

"What it means! Well, young man, your impudence beats the devil. Why, haven't we proved you a spy, by catching you in company with that sneaking scoundrel, Bill Woodworth?"

"Bill Woodworth!" said Bob, showing a fair degree of surprise, I don't know any such man. If you mean him who has just left us, I was taken prisoner by him a short time since, in company with a crowd of others, and he said he intended to take me to Captain Higley's headquarters."

"I don't believe your story, young man," said the officer, "but if it is true, that Bill Woodworth is the most impudent, as well as the most daring scoundrel unhung."

The men who had followed Woodworth, returned, and reported that they could not find the slightest trace of the spy. The party then returned to the camp at a walk, two of them guarding our hero.

CHAPTER IX.

Brant Imprisoned and Paroled.

ARRIVED at the camp, Bob Brant was promptly conveyed by his captors to the office of the Provost-Marshal, an official upon whose tender mercies he put but little reliance. The officer gave his account of the affair, relating the suspicious circumstances in which he had found our hero. Bob was graciously permitted to give his version, and promptly stated that his name was Henry Errington, that he had come there with letters from some of their friends in the North, for the purpose of supplying small arms, percussion caps, and such material to the army; that he ran great risk in so doing, and thought it hard that he should be put to trouble and inconvenience on account of a person whom he had never seen before. He stated that he had finished his business at the camp, and was walking along the road, when he was met by a crowd of men whom he supposed to be patrolmen or rangers, headed by the man Woodworth, or whoever he was, who had arrested him on some suspicion; that Woodworth, or whoever he was, said that he was going to take him to Captain Higley's headquarters; and had stopped to search him for arms, when the cavalrymen came in sight, and the fellow darted off into the wood.

Bob told his story with an air of candor that sat well upon him, but it was evident that he would find no believers there.

"This is a strange story, young man," said the Provost, "one of the strangest stories I ever heard. In fact, it is entirely too strange to be true. Even old Bill Woodworth wouldn't have the impudence and the audacity to perpetrate such a trick: and what could be his motive in doing it, and how could he get the men to follow him?"

"Of his motive," answered Brant, "I know nothing, unless it may have been to rob me; but as for the men, it is evident that he had made them drunk, as they were all pretty full when I met them."

"Why did he go along with you alone, and what became of the other men?"

"He sent the other men on, to look up more stragglers, as he said, and told them to stop at the first whisky shop and take a drink, and that Captain Higley would pay for it."

The Provost was getting indignant.

"There is no such man as Captain Higley," said he. "Your story is utterly ridiculous, young man. Guard, search him."

Brant was accordingly subjected to a thorough search, and glad enough was he that he had got well rid of the plans and memoranda he had given to old Bill Woodworth, and that that individual had got safely off with them. Nothing was found upon him but his pistol, and one of the letters of introduction he had brought from Paducah. The latter evidently disposed the officer to look upon his case rather more favorably, and to think that there might be some truth in his representations. Nevertheless, he told our hero that he must commit him for further examination; though, as he appeared to be a gentleman, and might be found "all right," he would not put him in the common guard-house, but would lodge him for the night in the calaboose or town jail.

Bob asked to be confronted with General Cheatham, expressing himself as certain that that officer would order his immediate release, but he was informed that the General could not be seen at that hour, and he must consequently be content to remain in the prison for the night. His pistol was then taken from him, but he was allowed to retain the money he had about him, and was marched off to the calaboose, under a guard.

There were few spectators at the Provost-Marshal's office; but young Brant had noticed among them the shining countenance of old Pharaoh, who had glanced at him significantly. When he was taken to the jail, he observed that the old negro followed him at a short distance, and, just before the door closed upon him, he again caught the significant glance of Pharaoh.

Bob Brant was ushered into a small room, hardly to be called a cell, in which he was alone. It was a comfortable enough room, for a jail, but Bob felt painfully that it *was* a jail, a place which, at that time, he most heartily wished himself out of. No thought of personal danger entered his mind, for he was sure that no proof could be found against him, unless old Bill Woodworth should be caught, of which he had no fear, or unless Major Mercer should inform against him, an idea which he rejected as soon as it presented itself. But he had promised, and the General expected him, to be inside of Fort Donelson within four days, and he felt that he ought to have started that night, or in the morning at farthest, in order to arrange his plans for getting in and out again. He knew that it would hardly be possible for him to get a hearing before noon the next day, and even then he would not be likely to get clear without further detention, so that he saw little chance of being in the promised place at the promised time.

The calaboose, as Bob had previously noticed from the outside, was a strong building, substantially built of heavy hewn timbers, and on the inside he found it stoutly double planked, the planks being spiked to the timbers. He soon saw the hopelessness of any attempt at escape, and settled down into a fit of the blues. Thoughts of Mabel Mercer mixed themselves up gloomily with the unpleasant web of his perplexities, and he became so restless and uneasy that he was unable to sleep, but walked the floor with moody brow and downcast eye.

It was hardly an hour after our hero had been lodged in the jail, that a young gentleman in the uniform of a Confederate Captain, evidently inebriated, came walking unsteadily along the street, and "brought up" in front of the sentry who stood at the jail door. The sentry gave the usual salute to the officer, and the latter, steadying himself against the post, addressed him as follows:

"Did they bring a young chap in here a while ago, from the Provost's office?"

"Yes, sir."

"Let me in; I want to see him."

"Can't do it, Captain; it's against orders."

"I reckon General Cheatham's orders are good enough for you," said the officer, taking a bit of paper from his pocket. "Here, young man, can you read writing? Let me read it for you, though," and he read:

"Henry Errington is paroled until further orders, on condition that he keeps within the quarters of Captain Hemingway.

"By order of BRIG. GEN. CHEATHAM.
"R. A. COOLEY, A. A. Gen."

"There, young man, you see that signature, do you? I want to see if this young man is the one the General means, and if he is, he goes to my quarters to-night."

"All right, Captain," said the obsequious sentry, as he opened the door, and called to those within to admit the visitor to the new prisoner.

CHAPTER X.

Charley Mercer and Brant.

YOUNG Brant was surprised when this bearded and mustached officer walked into his cell, and he stared blankly at him. The visit, however, was a relief to his monotony, and served to distract his attention from his own thoughts.

The officer closed the door carefully.

"Good evening, Mr. Errington," said he; "how do you find yourself?"

"Pretty well, I thank you, for a man who is locked up. Hope you are in good health yourself."

"Yes, I am well enough; always am, Robert."

"You have slightly mistaken my name," said Bob, without moving a muscle. "My name is Henry Errington, not Robert."

"Reckon it isn't, just now," said the officer, as he pulled off his heavy, dark beard and moustache, and disclosed the smooth face and laughing eyes of Charley Mercer.

"Why, Mercer, you're welcome as ice in the dog-days. How did you get in?"

"Walked in, of course; and now, without any more talking, you will please just walk out with me, and I will tell you about it afterward. Old Pharaoh is waiting near the corner of our lane with a couple of horses and your traps, and you can be far away from this before sun-up."

"All right," said Bob, reserving his wonder; "have you a scrap of paper about you?"

2   5

Charley Mercer tore off the blank part of a letter, and Bob hurriedly scrawled the following lines on it in pencil:

"IN THE CALABOOSE, Wednesday night.
"GEN. CHEATHAM:

"After risking my life to serve the Confederacy, I thought I was entitled to better treatment. I am not pleased with this lodging, and have concluded to quit it. I have business which calls me to Fort Donelson, from which place I will write to you, and if you wish me to carry out the contract I made with you, will arrange for the delivery of the arms, etc.

"Please give my respects to the Provost-Marshal, and tell him to be careful not to pick up the wrong man next time.

"Yours, very respectfully,
"HENRY ERRINGTON."

This precious document the young man left in a place where it could be easily found in the morning, and followed his guide, who by this time had resumed his beard and his unsteady gait.

As they passed out of the door, the pretended Confederate officer said to the sentry: "It's all right, young man. This is the chap I was looking for. I tell you the General was hopping mad when he heard that he had been locked up in the jail."

"All right, Captain," replied the soldier, as he saluted.

"Come along, old boy," said Charley, hilariously, as he took his companion by the arm. "We'll make a night of it at my quarters, and I'll get you so tight that you won't be able to break your parole if you want to; and if I get in the same fix, guard duty may go to the devil, if I get cashiered for it."

When they were out of hearing of the thoroughly deceived sentry, walking swiftly along the street, Bob Brant thought he could indulge his curiosity, and asked his friend:

"How, in the name of common sense, did you get that parole from the General?"

"Didn't get any parole from the General," said the laughing boy; "made it myself. And that reminds me that I had better destroy it."

He accordingly tore it in small pieces, and scattered them along the roadside.

"Made it yourself! You are very rash, and have been bringing yourself into danger for my sake. Don't you know that it would be as much as your life is worth, if you should be found out?"

"But how is any one ever going to know any thing about it? Why, you yourself could not recognize me in this dress and with this beard, and I am sure that that sentry, who never saw me before, could not identify me."

"How did you come by that Confederate uniform?"

"Old Pharaoh stole it for me. It was one of the neatest things you ever saw. I tell you, there is a heap of come-out in that old nigger, whenever he chooses to let himself out."

"I should think so; and not a little in you, also. But I am sorry to see you risking your life for my sake—your life, that is so dear to your father and mother, and—your sister."

"Never mind my sister," said Charley Mercer, with a merry twinkle in his eye. "She put me up to this thing, though to be sure I didn't need any coaxing—the joke was too good a one to be lost. Old Pharaoh saw you going to the Provost-Marshal's office. He knew something was up, and followed and watched you until you were lodged in the jail, when he hurried home to bring us the news. He told no one but sister Mabel, however, and she told me, and, between the three of us, we soon fixed up a plan to get you out of there. Pharaoh said he knew where he could lay his hands, easily enough, on a Captain's coat, pants and cap, and that is the rig I am in now. Think I shall keep the suit—may find it useful some time. But you must get away from here, and which way do you want to go?"

Bob then told his friend of his desire to reach Fort Donelson as soon as possible; of his trouble, while in the jail, because he feared he would be unable to accomplish his mission, and of his present perplexity concerning getting in the fort, and—what was of greater importance—getting out again.

Charley Mercer said nothing, but ruminated. As they walked along briskly, though silently, they soon reached the corner of the lane, where, turning into a little piece of wood, they found old Pharaoh awaiting them with two saddled horses. The old African's eyes sparkled, and his face fairly glistened, as our hero and his guide walked up to him, and he expressed his satisfaction audibly:

"The Lord and all his holy angels bless you, Massa Brant! I knowed Massa Charley would fix the trick for you. Hi! he's too much for them 'Federates, and this ole nigger ain't nobody's chicken, neither. Won't Miss Mabel be glad when she knows how this thing come out? oh, no, guess not. Now, Massa Charles, you must hurry up to the house and take them clothes off, right straight 'way, and you mustn't wake nobody up. Needn't be 'feard of wakin' up Miss Mabel, I reckon, for I 'spect she hain't slept nary wink this blessed night."

Bob Brant's eyes twinkled, too, and he felt better all over, though his face became suddenly hot, and he was rather wet about the eyes.

As for Charley Mercer, he still seemed lost in thought, and made no answer to Pharaoh. At last he condescended to speak:

"Mr. Brant, here is your carpet-bag; are any of your clothes marked?"

"Of course not."

"All right, then. If you have any letters or writing of any kind, you had better destroy every thing as you go along. Now jump on this horse, and make as fast time as you please. Pharaoh will go with you as far as Uncle Tom's, and put you right on the way. I must stay here to-morrow, to see if this matter blows over. On the turnpike, near Dover, is a sort of a tavern, at a cross-roads, kept by a fellow named Michael Curwin. You can find it easily enough, and within four days I will meet you there. That's settled. By the way, could you give a fellow the oath of allegiance?"

"I am sorry to say, my dear boy, that I am not authorized to administer the oath."

"Then I will administer it myself. Now hear me: I do solemnly swear, before high Heaven, that I will bear true allegiance to the United States of America, and will use my utmost efforts to restore the Federal Union, and to maintain it against all its foes, whether foreign or domestic, at whatever risk or danger to life or fortune. So help me God!"

"There, be off with you, and remember Curwin's tavern."

"A moment, Charley," said Brant, pressing his friend's hand, and looking down, as he pretended to adjust his stirrups, "may I ask you to give my love to your sister?"

"Of course you may, and I will be glad to do it; and, if it will do you any good, I can assure you that she will be glad to receive it. Good-by; good-by, Pharaoh."

"Good-by," said Bob, "God bless you, and keep you safe!"

The white and black man, so strangely allied, turned their horses into the road, and were soon lost to the sight, as they disappeared over the hill, while Charley Mercer hurried homeward.

CHAPTER XI.

Hospitalities at Curwin's Tavern.

CURWIN'S tavern, on the Dover road, was never an inviting place, and, at the time of which we write, was less so than ever. The proprietor had, to be sure, done a very good business of late—more than could be expected of so small and uncomfortable a hostelrie—but on several occasions he had had a portion of his stock confiscated for selling whisky to the Confederate soldiers, and his reverses of fortune had not had the effect of sweetening his temper, which was never one of the most cheerful.

The house was a two-story affair, but was a miserable old rattle-trap, one of the "balloon" style, through the many cracks and crevices of which the wind whistled and howled as it pleased. A substantial log cabin was attached to the premises, which was used as a barn; but there was only a small portion of the roof remaining. In fact, the whole establishment, and the whole household, from old Curwin himself, down to a bare-legged and hatless little negro boy, looked dilapidated and "shiftless," to use the expressive Yankee word.

But, comfortless as it looked, the place appeared pleasant to Bob Brant, as he rode up to the door, on the evening of a chilly, misty, drizzling day. He was wet through, and it seemed as if the cold north-east wind had found its way into the marrow of every bone. The enticing placards which adorned the window, announcing the various kinds of liquors to be found within, were a grateful sight, and a glimpse, through the open kitchen door, of the preparations for supper, was still more agreeable. His horse, also, seemed glad at the prospect of rest and food, and testified his approbation by a shrill, exultant neigh, which soon brought old Curwin himself to the door. Calling a young negro to take care of our hero's horse, he invited him to alight and enter. Bob was not slow to accept the invitation, and followed his gruff-looking landlord into the house, carrying his carpet-bag with him.

He had first taken care, however, to secure about his person a brace of pistols, which old Pharaoh had thoughtfully put in his holsters.

"A bad night, stranger," said old Curwin, as he closed the door after his guest.

"Yes," said Bob, as he laid down his little baggage, "a bad night, and I am glad I am out of it."

"Nice horse that of your'n. Should say he's a good beast."

"Yes, a good horse to go, and to stand up to his work. Wish you'd make your boy rub him down well."

"Oh, he's up to that, the boy is. That nigger likes a good hoss better'n he does his vittles, which is sayin' a heap for a nigger. 'Spect ye've rode purty fur to-day, stranger?"

"Not so very far; but I lost the road."

"And whar mout ye be goin' to?"

"I am going here just now," said Brant, who was not at all pleased at the landlord's inquisitiveness, and who saw the necessity of changing the conversation or quieting his interrogator. "Landlord, can you make me something hot to warm me up, as I am too nearly frozen to talk."

"Give ye some hot whisky, with sugar into it," said Curwin, as he bustled about to prepare the fluids. "That's purty much all we've got now."

"Perhaps," said Bob, anxious to get in the good graces of his host, as he looked around and saw three or four men sitting in the partial light by the fire, "perhaps these gentlemen will take something."

As usual in that latitude, the "gentlemen" he referred to "didn't care if they did," and they stepped up with an alacrity which might induce the belief that they were glad to be invited, while old Curwin's face looked almost pleasant at the prospect of custom.

While the landlord was mixing the spirits to suit the varied tastes of "the crowd," young Brant looked around to see into what kind of company he had fallen.

"At the first glance, his eyes, though at first he could not believe them, fell upon the never-to-be-forgotten face of old Bill Woodworth, who was leaning stiffly against the counter, stirring his toddy with a spoon. Bob started involuntarily, and the landlord noticed it.

"What's the matter now, stranger?" said he, eyeing the young man suspiciously. "Any thin' scart ye?"

Brant's presence of mind returned at the instant.

"By Jove," he replied, "that picture on the wall looks like a girl I once knew."

He then walked up to the picture he mentioned, a cheap lithograph, and gazed intently at it for a few minutes, while he collected his thoughts and recovered from his astonishment.

While the "gentlemen" were imbibing, Bob observed that Woodworth took no notice of him, and of course concluded that it was expected that neither should recognize the other. As he took a seat by the fire, and called for cigars for "the crowd," he had an opportunity of inspecting his late acquaintance more closely. Old Bill was transformed greatly as to dress, though it seemed that his shape and countenance could not be altered. He was attired in clothes that would be called fine in that region, though by no means fashionably cut, held a heavy whip in his hand, the lash of which he kept passing through his fingers, and looked what Bob thought to be the very picture of a substantial Kentucky or Tennessee farmer.

It was old Bill Woodworth, without doubt. There was no mistaking the flash of that keen eye, or the determination expressed by those thin lips. But how came he there? How had he made his way to Cairo, and got back into that country so quickly? Above all, how did he dare to be there at all? These were question which puzzled the young man not a little, but, as he did not think it worth while to perplex himself about what he could not comprehend, he became content in the belief that the old scout knew what he was about, and that he would always be found in the right place at the right time.

The men around the fire had been talking quite freely when Brant came in, but after his entrance they had been nearly silent, only exchanging a few words about the weather or the prospect of supper.

The landlord edged his chair up to the fire, which he stirred. He seemed uneasy about something, and at last he said, looking at our hero.

"A bad night agin, stranger. Wot makes you all so dull?"

"It is dull," said Bob, aroused from his revery. "Landlord, give us some more drinks all around."

This, by way of parenthesis, was a course of conduct that we would not recommend to a judicious young man in Brant's peculiar position. He was rather too clever for the occasion, and, although his patronage tended to appease old Curwin, yet the suspicions of that faithful servant of King Jefferson were awakened by the circumstance. However, he bestirred himself to procure the fluids, and the faces of the rest of the party, except that of Woodworth, sensibly brightened.

When the landlord had brought the glasses, he again seated himself, and turned his gray eyes upon Brant, his hands resting upon his knees, and his countenance expressive of suspicion.

"Stranger," said he, "I don't like to be too curious about a gen'leman as spends his money free like you, but these is ticklish times, and my house is watched purty close, and I think it's my duty to know who the men are as comes here, and whar they come from, and whar they're goin' to. Now, that's jest wot I want to know about you."

"It seems to me, landlord," replied Bob, "that you are running your ideas of duty into the ground. For my part, I am not in the habit of satisfying idle curiosity. I am traveling on my own business, and what that business is, is nobody's business but my own. If I am asked by any authorized officer, I will tell it, but do not intend to make it known to every one-horse tavern keeper I meet."

"You talk brash enough, young man, but your talk won't go down with old Mike Curwin. I want to know, now, whether you're for the Confederacy or not."

"You may bet on that."

"Then you can't object to tellin' me which way you're a-goin'."

"Going my way."

"Now, landlord," spoke up one of the men, "I don't see the use of botherin' the young feller, when he says he's for the Confederacy, and spends his money like a white man."

Curwin glanced angrily at him.

"You'd better dry up, John Gasher; you're nothin' but a no'count Kentucky skunk, nohow, and ye mout get your ownself into a scrape."

The man made no further objection, but Bob saw that he would have a chance in a "scrimmage," and spoke sharply to the landlord.

"No more talk is necessary. I do not consider myself bound to satisfy your curiosity, and do not intend to do it."

Curwin sprung from his seat, and made a rush at our hero, but was met by the muzzle of one of Colt's six-inch barrels, pointed at his breast. Bob glanced at Woodworth, who was still amusing himself with drawing the lash of his whip through his fingers.

Curwin stepped back for his gun. As he took it from the rack, Brant raised his left arm, levelled his pistol over the elbow, and sighted along the barrel.

"If you raise that gun," he said, calmly, "I will bore a hole through you. Please move your arm a little, so that I may have a fair sight at that third button."

Curwin was brave, or desperate, enough, but the appearance of the "situation" did not please him. He appealed to the "crowd."

"Men, do you stand this? Is a loyal citizen, who is only a-doin' of his duty, to be run over by a young chap as is perobably a nigger-stealin' spy?"

Woodworth, at whom Curwin looked, was still fingering the lash of his whip.

"Wa-a-l, landlord," said he, "I don't see as you've any call to question the stranger so close and perticlar like."

Another of the party was fingering for a knife, and moved closer to the fire and to our hero. But Bob's quick eye noticed that old Bill Woodworth had changed his hand, bringing it nearer to the heavy butt of the whip, and as he felt secure from a flank attack in that quarter, he maintained a steady aim at the landlord.

Affairs were in this position, Curwin standing irresolute, with his gun in his hand, Brant still sighting his pistol at the third button on his coat, the man with the knife edging toward Brant, and Woodworth grasping firmly the stock of his whip and compressing his lips, when the door suddenly opened.

CHAPTER XII.

An Opportune Arrival.

"HALLOO! what's the row here?" said the new comer, with a merry laugh, as he closed the door hastily. "Any chance for a free fight here, landlord?"

Young Brant immediately recognized the voice and the laugh, as those peculiar to Charley Mercer, but he did not take his eye or his pistol off of Curwin, until the latter laid aside his gun, and addressed the seeming officer, as he touched his hat.

"Why, Captin, it is jest a stranger as is come in here, and he won't give no account of himself, and that's suspicious, as you must allow, as folks as won't give no account of themselves is perobably Yankee spies or something wuss. He sorter got the whip hand of me jest now; but I'd hev brort him to his milk purty quick ef you hadn't come in, and now I'll turn the cuss over to you."

"Which is the man?" said Charley, glancing around.

"That yere feller with the pistil."

"What, Heffernan!" exclaimed Charley, stepping up to Brant and laying his hand upon his shoulder. "The very man I have been looking for. Landlord, you have done exactly right; and you deserve a great deal of credit for your caution and your devotion to the Confederacy. I will see that it is represented in the proper quarter. This man is a deserter from my company, Company B, Fourth Arkansas regiment, and I am glad to get hold of him."

"There," said Curwin, triumphantly, appealing to "the crowd," "I knowed thar war su'thin' wrong about that chap. I'm never out of the way when my eyes light onto a feller."

"All right, landlord," replied the officer: "but I think there is not really any harm in this man. He is true and sound, but he wanted a furlough to go and see his girl, up in Kentucky, and the Colonel refused it, and this scapegrace took French leave and furloughed himself."

The deserter had now looked up and scrutinized his captor. Mercer was again attired in the uniform of a Confederate Captain, and his apparent age was increased by a heavy dark mustache.

Bob was quick to take his cue, and said to the officer, rather doggedly, but carelessly:

"I was just on my way to join the regiment, Captain, and to receive whatever punishment might be inflicted on me. It was tyrannical in the Colonel to refuse me a furlough, and I was bound to see the girl, if I died for it."

"Well, Heffernan, don't bother your brains about it. The Colonel understands the matter, and I am on the right side of him, and I think you will get off with a short imprisonment, and the loss of any pay that is coming to you."

"Wa-a-l, now," said Curwin, "I'm glad to hear it ain't no wuss, though the young feller was sassy enough to me. If he's true

to the cause, I sh'd be sorry to see such a likely chap shot, when we've a-needin' of soldiers. Come, Captin and gents, all of you take suthin' with me. P'raps it will cheer ye up, young feller."

The request was generally acceded to, and Charley Mercer then asked the landlord to hurry up supper, which was speedily put on the table, and all ate it, such as it was, with a hearty relish. While at the table, Mercer again opened his conversational batteries upon his deserter.

"Well, Heffernan, you must have been in a hurry to get back, as you borrowed a horse in Kentucky."

"I intended to send it home, Captain, the first chance I could get."

"I suppose you did, but as I am here now, and must carry you into Donelson for safe keeping to-morrow, I will have to return it for you myself, unless I can find some one to take the job off my hands."

"I am goin' down Kentuck way," said Woodworth, who had been doing full duty with his knife and fork, "and if it ain't much outer my track, I will take the hoss along for yer."

"Very well; you appear to be a respectable man, and I will trust you. Let me know when you start."

"I shall start to-night, Capting, and as I'll hev a hoss of my own under me, I can lead that yere animule as well as not."

"Heffernan," said Charley, "I understand you borrowed a pair of pistols with the horse. I suppose you will want to return them also."

"Here they are," said Bob, as he handed up his weapons to Mercer, who delivered them to Woodworth, requesting him to put them in the holsters.

When the meal was finished, Woodworth "allowed" that he was ready to start, and went out. Young Mercer followed him to the door, and the two had a few words of private chat, after which, Charley reëntered the house, and seated himself by the fire. The steps of the two horses were soon heard passing the house.

"Do you know that old chap, Captin?" said Curwin to Mercer.

"I know him by reputation as a farmer, and a man of means. I don't think he would be guilty of stealing a horse."

"I 'spect not, for he would find that a risky business around here. 'Pears to me I've seen that man some'eres, but I can't rightly place him."

Charley then told the landlord that he should want a single room for himself and his prisoner, which was obtained, after some difficulty, rooms being scarce in the "hotel," and the two retired to bed. Bob wished to ask his friend a few questions, particularly about old Bill Woodworth's appearance there, and more particularly about Mabel Mercer; but Charley did not seem disposed to talk, and our hero repressed his curiosity, and soon fell into a sound sleep.

In the morning, after they had taken their breakfast and paid their score, the two started out afoot, on their way to the fort. As it was a long walk, they had sufficient opportunity for explanations and other conversation. Brant first asked his friend how old Woodworth happened to be there, and how he dared to be in that locality.

"That is more than I can tell you," was the answer. "I never saw the man before, but Pharaoh described him to me so exactly, that I knew him as soon as I met him. As he left, he told me to say to you that he would not be far away from here, and that he would try to help you if he could. Pharaoh says that the old man is a witch, and can do any thing."

"I have great confidence in him, also, for he is the most inevitable and ubiquitous individual I ever saw. But I am at a loss to know how he is going to help me to get out of that fort, for I suppose you intend taking me in."

"Of course, being a stranger, I must take you in, and as for getting out, you must trust to luck and your own wits, for I shall not venture in again. My uniform will do very well for a while, as no one there knows any thing about the Fourth Arkansas, and I can tell them all about it, but it would be too dangerous to risk it again, as it is very likely I might meet some one who knows me. Here are some letters which old Pharaoh got for me from the real deserter. You must read them over, and make up as pitiful a tale as you can, and I do not doubt that you will have a good enough chance to look around. That Pharaoh is a first-class hand to steal, and I shall be almost afraid to trust him about the farm any more."

"Never fear about my getting out, after I am once well in. Now, tell me if my escapade from Jackson caused any excitement."

"Very little. The Provost-Marshal was angry enough, and the sentry was put under arrest; but when the General saw your note, he laughed, and said it was cleverly done. He told the Provost to take no further steps in the matter, as he was sorry the arrest had been made, and had no doubt that you would turn up again after a while. 'These Yankees,' said he, 'will not be caught playing spies, when they can make money in other ways.' The matter dropped much easier than I thought it would. I heard the particulars from an officer on the General's staff."

Satisfied upon these points, Brant then asked Charley concerning his family, hoping to hear something about Mabel. He was not disappointed, but had the gratification of learning that she had expressed great anxiety concerning his safety, and had enjoined it upon Charley to do all he could for him, and persuade him to leave the dangerous employment in which he was engaged. Bob felt as if he would be willing to give it up at any moment, if Mabel Mercer would promise to console him for his broken resolution. Young Mercer also told him that the Major had been making preparations for moving up into Kentucky, and would probably change his residence immediately.

His curiosity being satisfied, our hero applied himself to reading the package of letters which Charley had given him, in order to "post himself up" in his new character, and shortly after he had finished his reading, they were challenged by a Confederate picket. Mercer, who, for the time being, was Captain Kirby, of the Fourth Arkansas regiment, soon made known his business, and the two friends were escorted to the fort, where they were conducted to the office of the Provost-Marshal, an establishment which Bob, as yet, was unable to enter without experiencing a strange sensation about his throat.

"Captain Kirby" produced a pass for himself, signed by Colonel Burden, of the Fourth Arkansas regiment, and explained the circumstances under which he had arrested "Thomas Heffernan," a deserter from that regiment, whom he then and there produced. He told substantially the same story he had told at Curwin's tavern, and Bob, being appealed to, gave a pitiful but manly narrative of his escapade, which strongly disposed the officer in his favor.

"As I had business in this direction," said Mercer, "the Colonel gave me a furlough, and said that while I was here, he would like me to look up this young man and bring him back to camp, and I was to tell him that if he would come quietly and promise good behavior in future, his punishment would be very light, if any thing. I have some important business up the river, and would like to leave him in your care until I return, say for four or five days, when I will have transportation for him to go to camp with me. I am fully convinced, that when I found him, he was endeavoring to make his way back to camp, and as he is one of the best men in the regiment, I can trust him. I think it, therefore, entirely unnecessary to confine him, if he will give his promise not to attempt to escape."

The officer replied that if Captain Kirby was satisfied, he was, and that Heffernan might have his parole. Bob accordingly agreed to this very satisfactory arrangement, assuring the "gentleman from Arkansas," that he would find him there on his return, which was certainly near enough to the truth.

The *soi-disant* Captain Kirby then took his departure, pleading the importance of his business and the shortness of his furlough as an excuse for his haste, and our hero was again alone in a strange place, and among men hostile to his flag and himself.

CHAPTER XIII.

Brant's Escape and Recapture.

BOB BRANT had a ready tongue, was plentifully supplied with tact, and knew well how to adapt himself to circumstances. He made good use of these talents, and the consequence was, that, so far from being confined, or looked upon as a dangerous character, he was allowed the liberty of the fort and intrenchments, and was treated with more consideration than he could have expected under the most favorable circumstances. The men in whose company he was thrown, looked upon him as a sort of hero, as a martyr to love, and generally praised his "pluck." The officers, also, whom he met, treated him with respect, as a man of intelligence and education, especially as his military training, enabled him, in his walks about the fortifications, to point out and show them how to remedy some trifling defects in the works and in the position and management of the guns, which had been overlooked by the superior officers.

This was done in a modest and unobtrusive manner, that gained him friends and procured him facilities that he would not otherwise have had.

In short, he was well treated, and could have been contented, had it not been that it was necessary for him to get away from there, and that speedily. He was satisfied with his experience of the inside of the fort, as he had gained all the information he wished, and now he greatly desired to see the outside. On the afternoon of the day after he had been brought in, he concluded that he had no more business there, and that it would be safe, as well as more profitable to leave.

Therefore, he concluded to bid adieu to Fort Donelson, until he could reënter it under the protection of the Stars and Stripes.

But how was it to be done? He saw that the attempt was dangerous, but he did not puzzle his brain long before he decided on the best way to make it. He might easily have obtained the countersign, and might probably have passed out unquestioned, but he was convinced that it could not be long before he would be stopped or overtaken. He knew that he must leave at night and by stealth. At the eastern angle of the principal work he had noticed that a heavy gun had been recently placed, and that the earth had shelved away from the embankment, leaving a considerable space below the gun, and half filling the ditch. He had also noticed that the fallen trees and masses of brushwood were thicker opposite this angle than elsewhere, and that the distance to the woods was less, thus affording the best chance for concealment during his escape, and for a cover when the escape was effected. He resolved to attempt to leave by that avenue, and to make the attempt that night.

Accordingly, watching a time when he could be alone, he made a few condensed memoranda, and sketched a plan of the works and guns, upon a small scrap of paper as would contain them, and concealed it under the insole of his boot. He remembered the fate of Major André, but concluded that that unfortunate officer had no insole to his boot.

This done, he wandered about the barracks, and accepted several invitations to partake surreptitiously, of the extract of corn, of which he appeared to drink very freely, so much so, that he was cautioned of the danger of taking too much. But, despite the caution, he permitted so much of the enticing fluid to get into his head, that (I grieve to say it, but as a faithful chronicler am obliged to record it,) when "taps" struck, he was disinclined to take the trouble to undress, and fell upon his bunk, with not only his coat but his boots on. His mates in the log hut thought him a good subject for jokes, and exhausted their wit upon him, the best attempt being

"—— Now lies he there,
And none so poor to do him reverence,"

until they also dropped off to sleep.

When this occurred, a change came over the spirit of Brant's dream, if any dream he had had. The fumes of the liquor seemed to affect him no longer, and his movements were those of a man with a clear head and steady nerves. He sat up, looked about, moved lightly around the room, as if to satisfy himself that his room-mates were indeed asleep, then put on his hat and stepped lightly out of the door.

The night was cloudy and dark, and as he breathed the cool, damp air, he almost felt free. He moved silently and stealthily along the outer edge of the log huts, occasionally slipping around to the inner side of one, as he saw a sentinel approaching, until he reached the angle which he desired to find. Then, stepping quickly from the shadow of a hut, he reached the heavy gun which had lately been mounted at this angle, and crouched by the side of its carriage. From this position he peered out, and saw a sentinel approaching by the side of the parapet, at a measured pace. Bob speedily ensconced himself under the gun, lying lengthwise with it, and identifying himself with the mass of iron, so that he could not be observed in the darkness. Here he lay, scarcely daring to breathe, until the sentinel passed, within a few feet of him, whistling as he went by. As soon as this man was well out of the way, Bob slipped down into the ditch, and clambered up on the other side. He knew that it would be fully ten minutes before the sentinel returned to that spot, and accordingly crawled upon his hands and knees for a few rods through the fallen trees and brush, until he found shelter under the withered leaves of a tree-top, where he hid and awaited for the return of the sentinel.

He had not long to wait, for soon he again heard the measured step and the low whistle, and again knew that it had passed by. Again he worked his way, slowly and toilsomely, through the debris, until he stopped at another cover. He had not been exactly quick enough, however, for the soldier, as he returned, caught the sound of a rustling in the brush, and stopped and looked.

"Who goes there?" rung from the fort.

Bob lay quiet. He was well concealed, and all was silent.

"Some kind of a varmint, I reckon," muttered the sentinel, and resumed his solitary walk and his whistling.

In this way Bob wormed himself along, until he was sure that he was out of sight or hearing of the fort. It was slow work, and was hard work, but liberty was ahead, and more than liberty, the honor of his flag, the glory of his country, the cause of the Union. He thought of this, and, above all, it must be confessed, he thought of Mabel Mercer, and resolved to be cautious while he was bold. Therefore, he still picked his way carefully, but quietly, until he reached a clear space, a short distance from the timber, when he ran for the protection of the standing trees.

Once under their shade, he breathed more freely, but he was again perplexed. As the night was dark, and he had only a very general idea of distances and directions, he did not know what course to strike. He had no time to spare for consideration, and pushed out boldly, keeping near the edge of the timber, and trusting to luck to hit some road. He walked rapidly, and partly ran, taking care not to stumble, or to make any unnecessary noise. He knew that he would be obliged to pass the Confederate pickets, but as he had learned, while in the fort, the approximate position of the picket line, he had little fear on that score. After a while he espied a faint light to the right, whereupon he made a detour a short distance to the left, and pursued his way more carefully and silently, until he had left the light well to his right and rear, when he again hurried forward more rapidly and boldly than before. Thus he continued for more than an hour, and had begun to wonder when, if ever, he was to find his way out, when he came to a clear space, and perceived the dim outline of a house a short distance ahead. Of course, where there was a house, there must be a road, and Brant considered that his best plan would be to make for the building.

When he reached it, it was soon evident that it was no other than the "hotel" of

Michael Curwin, at which he had stopped two nights before. Our hero was surprised to learn that he had traveled in that direction, but was glad that he now knew where he was, and that he could see his way clear. Jumping over the low fence, he found himself in the main road, and stepped on rapidly, as he had been over the road before, without experiencing any difficulty. He knew that if he was missed from the fort in the morning, it would probably be a considerable time before his absence would be noticed, and felt confident that he could get out of harm's way before pursuit would be made.

He had proceeded about a quarter of a mile, when he came to a small road or lane, which led off to the left. Here he stopped, to meditate a moment on the proper course to pursue. The stop was fatal, for there was a quick rush from a thicket at the side of the road, and, before Brant could look around, he was seized by the arms behind his back, and, despite his struggles, these useful members of his body were speedily and strongly bound in that position.

CHAPTER XIV.

The Captive Rescued.

"WELL, I've caught ye, hev I?" was the first exclamation he heard.

His captor then stepped in front of him, and Brant saw, to his dismay, that it was old Curwin himself. His ugly features were tortured into a hideous grin, and his gray eyes shone with satisfaction from under their shaggy brows. By his side stood a grinning darkey boy, apparently fourteen or fifteen years old.

Bob was not pleased; in fact, he was terribly disgusted with the situation of affairs. He was more than disgusted—he was absolutely alarmed—for he felt sure that this old sinner would carry him to the fort, and there deliver him up; and he also was sure that he was completely in his power, and had no chance of escaping, unless Providence should interfere; and once in the fort, he well knew what his fate would be. There came a sudden and dizzy rush of feeling over him, in which were mixed up the duty expected of him, the blessed old flag of his country, his father, his home, and Mabel Mercer, while beyond all, his

prophetic vision perceived a dangling rope, with an ominous noose at the end. But this feeling passed as soon as it came, and Bob braced himself up, resolved, if it came to the worst, to meet his fate like a man, but in the mean time to lose no opportunity in endeavoring to avert it.

"I've caught ye, hev I?" repeated Curwin, eyeing his prisoner with a look of malicious glee. "Thought ye was gettin' off mighty cute, didn't ye? Lucky I happened to be out late to-night, or I wouldn't hev lit on ye. My old eyes was sharp enough to' tell who ye was, as soon as I sot 'em on ye; and, thinks I, there's that ere deserter, if he ain't no wuss, a-makin' tracks for Yankee land; and this old coon laid for ye, he did, and got ye, too, ye dogoned ornary skunk!"

"You are entirely mistaken, sir," protested Bob. "I have left the fort on my parole, if you understand what that means, and was on my way to join my regiment."

"That won't do, young man. I've hearn such chaps as you say that sort of thing before now, for I've caught fellers as was desartin', and hev made suthin' out of 'em, too; and 'pears to me you told purty much the same story night afore last to the Captain, and the Captain took ye to the fort any how, and I reckon I'll do jist as he did. Do ye see any thin' green in my eye?"

"Not in this light," said Bob; "I haven't a good chance to look."

"Don't go to be sassy, young man, or it'll be worse for ye. I've got the whip hand of ye now, as ye had of me t'other night, and more, too, and I'm jist a-considerin', at this minit, whether I shall blow yer durned brains out, or take ye into the fort; but I reckon the fort'll win, as they pay well thar for your style. Now, jist you move along purty sharp, or I'll put ye whar ye won't stir yer legs again till judgment day."

The inducement of a pistol held to his head was sufficient to persuade Brant to do as his captor required, and the three started in the direction of the "hotel," old Curwin walking upon our hero's right, with his left hand upon his shoulder, while the right clenched a cocked pistol, and the negro boy shuffled along a little in advance, and to the left.

"At one moment, Bob thought of bribing this ardent patriot, but he recollected that he was in his power, and had no control over the money in his pocket, and instantly rejected the idea. But another thought struck him, and he was unwilling to miss any chance of regaining his liberty, now so valuable to him.

"Can you read?" said he, to the old man.

"Me read! Well, perhaps I could when I was younger'n I am now; but if I ever could, I've done forgot it. My old woman used to do my readin' and writin' for me, but she's gone dead, and now I don't want to do none. What do ye want to know fur?"

"Because, if you could read, I would show you a letter I have from the officer commanding the fort, giving me a pass to Arkansas."

Of course our hero could not be expected to confine himself strictly to the truth. It was not in his instructions that he should do so; in fact, his instructions tended quite the other way; and the commanders of the army of the Union, and through them, honest Abraham Lincoln, were responsible for any such slight misstatements as he might consider it necessary to make. Young Brant, however, did not pause to consider the matter in either a moral or an ethical point of view; he had hoped to impose upon Curwin's ignorance one of the letters to "Thomas Heffernan, private," as a genuine epistle from the commander of Fort Donelson, but the bait would not take.

"I rather reckon ye can't play any games on me," said Curwin, "and thar's no use in yer tryin' it on any more. I won't say that ye hain't got sech a letter, but if ye hev, I know I can't read it, and am sure they ken, at the fort; so ye may jest show it to 'em thar."

"Massa Mike," said the negro boy, "is dis gen'leman one o' dem Yankee Linkin's dat wants to steal us poor niggers?"

"I ain't quite sartin about that, Jake, though I don't think he's quite so bad as that."

"Lor, Massa Mike, I's mighty 'feard o' dem Yankee folks. What does they do wid de niggers wen dey cotch 'em?"

"They kills 'em and roasts 'em, Jake, and you may be thankful that you was borned in a country whar ye're took keer on, and whar ye hain't no call to be 'feard on 'em.

"I jest did thort I seed one ob 'em dis bery night, and I don't 'spect he's ever so far from here, neither."

As the boy said this, he threw a quick, but significant glance at our hero, who was

momentarily startled, and thought of old Bill Woodworth.

"Jest you hold yer yaup, youngster, or ye'll ketch a cowhidin' when ye git home."

Bob Brant thought that he saw a straw to catch at. Dropping suddenly upon one knee, he assumed an expression of pain, and exclaimed that there was something in his boot, which hurt his foot so that he was unable to walk. He requested his captor to loose his hands, that he might see what was the matter.

"No ye don't, young man," doggedly replied that worthy. "I 'spect this is some new trick ye've been a-gettin' up. But I don't want to be hard on ye, so jest sit down, and let this yere nigger pull off your boot."

Brant sat down, accordingly, and held out his foot to the boy, while Curwin bent over his shoulder, cursing very volubly. As the boy took hold of the boot, Bob thought, in an interval that occurred between the old man's curses, that he heard a step. He also noticed that the boy cast a glance down the road. But the sound, if any there was, did not continue, and Bob concluded that the wish was father to the thought.

The boot come off very slowly, but at last the boy, Jake, held it in his hand. Curwin leaned over to take it, and Brant thought he heard the step again. He was not mistaken this time, for the next instant he heard a dull, heavy sound, and his late landlord and present captor fell over him, and rolled on the ground.

Brant jumped up as quickly as his bound arms would permit him, and saw before him old Bill Woodworth, who stood looking at the fallen man, and holding a pistol by the barrel.

"The cussed critter!" said Woodworth, "I feel just as if I could run my knife through his dirty gizzard, and I would, too, ef it wasn't that I don't take naterally to murderin' fellow critters in cold blood, though it's nothin' more'n what they did to my poor boy, curse 'em! Here, Mr. Brant, let me onfasten these yere lashin's; I've got another use for 'em."

He proceeded to untie Brant's arms, and used the rope to fasten those of Curwin, who was still insensible from the effects of the blow that Woodworth had given him with the butt end of his pistol.

"A friend in need is a friend indeed," said Bob, as he grasped the rough hand of the ugly but honest patriot. I felt gloomy enough five minutes ago, though I hadn't given up hope, for I half believed you would turn up at the right place and time, and I have a pretty good knack at getting out of scrapes myself."

"Well," said Woodworth, "we'll do our talkin' some other time. Just now we must be for gettin' away from this. Here, Jake, help me carry this old wretch to the side of the road. He'll come to, purty soon, I reckon, and'll be meaner and sneakin'er, and more spitful'n ever."

With the assistance of the negro boy, who had been standing by with an expression of wonder and delight upon his sooty countenance, he deposited Curwin upon the grass at the roadside.

"Thar, now; them as he belongs to ken pick him up and cure his headache for him. 'Tain't anythin' to what he desarves. You, Jake"—the negro boy's eyes brightened—"the time I told ye about hes come, and I never split my word to no man, be he black or white, cept he's a traitor, and then I ken outlie the devil himself. Now, if ye want yer freedom, jest pick up that old man's pistol and come along i' us, and ye may bet yer wool he shan't flog ye agin. Ken ye shoot, young nigger?"

"Oh, yes, Massa Bill. I used to knock over de chickens when we had chickens, but 'pearslike I sh'd bo 'feard to shoot at a white man."

"Jake, these yere rebils ain't white men, by no manner of means. Ther hearts is a durned sight blacker'n your face ever darred to be; so ye ken jest shoot at 'em with a cl'ar conscience and a stiddy aim. Pick up that weepon and trot along."

The boy quickly did as he was desired, and, as he ran gayly before the two scouts, his nature seemed suddenly to have changed. He had lost his shuffling gait and hangdog look, and his step was light and springing, his countenance bright and cheerful. Woodworth noticed the change, and mentioned it to Brant, with a low, chuckling laugh.

"Do ye see that ar nigger, Mr. Brant? He ain't the boy he was a half hour ago—no, nor ten minutes ago, neither. Tell ye now, 'tain't so easy to fool these yere niggers as some folks think fur. They know a heap more'n they like to let on, and some on 'em has got so many secrets among 'em, that it's a wonder they don't bust. Thar mass'rs thinks they hes 'em fooled, but human natur is mighty desaivin', 'specially nigger natur. A nigger allus will be a nigger; thar's no

gittin' around that, but some on 'em has got a right smart notion of come-out to 'em. Now, I hain't knowed that nigger more'n two weeks, fur I haint been in this part of the kentry till lately, but he jest took to me at the first start, and he's done me some mighty good turns. I told him I'd pay him with his freedom, and now he thinks he's got it, as ye ken jedge by his looks and his actions. Mr. Brant, ef ye go into camp, as I s'pose ye will, for your life is too good and too young to be throwed away in this sort of work, and ye want a sarvant, jest freeze to that boy, and I'll be the warrant that he'll freeze to you."

After a few moments' rapid walking, old Bill turned a short distance into the wood, where two horses were discovered, tied to the tall trees. Brant recognized in one of them the animal which he had obtained from Charley Mercer, and which Woodworth had taken from Curwin's "hotel."

"You, Jake," said their guide, "do you know whar yer mass'r's hoss is?—old Mike's, I orter say, fer he ain't yer mass'r no longer."

"Oh, yes, Massa Bill; de hoss jest ober here in de field, 'cross de road."

"Then take this rope, and run and git him, and bring him here quicker'n lightnin'. 'Tain't no hoss stealin', mind ye," he continued, seeing the boy hesitate. "I jest confisticate that ar hoss, in the name of the United States of America and of old Abe Lincoln, *I* do; so jest you jump, wuss'n a squirrel!"

The boy disappeared like a flash of lightning, if so dark an object can be compared to lightning.

CHAPTER XV.

Journey of Brant and Woodworth.

"Now, Mr. Brant," said Woodworth, "gist hand over to me what papers you've got to send in; for I know the kentry, and ken git 'em to camp quicker'n you ken. Besides, when we fetch up whar we 'spect to rest to-night, I'm doubtin' whether ye'll car to go any further."

"I hope you do not suppose that a day's ride will tire me out," expostulated Bob. "I think I can stand as much as any man of my inches."

"P'raps ye ken; I ain't doubtin' about

that, but still I say what I do say, and I hev my reasons for sayin' it, too. But in my suckemstances, the papers are better off with me."

Bob pulled off his boot, and handed the scrap of paper to the old man, who carefully made a small opening in the lining of his boot, in which he placed the scrap, and then closed the aperture with some gum from a tree.

"Thar! ef they should ever take me alive, I don't think they'd hev that evidence agin me, though God knows they've got plenty more. Ye'll find yer pistils in them holsters, Mr. Brant, and ye'd better see ef they're all right. A keerful man allus looks keerfully to his weepons. Now let us git out of this."

The two untied and mounted their horses, and walked them out of the timber, into the road, where they met Jake coming up at a gallop, riding barebacked, and guiding his horse by the halter. As soon as he saw them, he commenced whooping and causing the animal he rode to prance and curvet.

"None of that, now, young darkey," said the old scout, "ye'd better stick to yer old .rainin' till ye ken git a better one. But remember that I'm yer mass'r now, till ye fotch up in the land of freedom, and then I reckon ye'd better sarve under old Abe Linkin, till ye larn how to take car of yerself. Ye can jest ride along quietly, behind us white folks, and keep at a 'spectful distance. Mind ye hev an eye out over yer shoulder, to see if all's right behind, and don't let me see no more of yer monkey shines."

The party then proceeded at a slow trot, Woodworth and Brant in the advance, with the boy, Jake, bringing up the rear. By this time the darkness was sensibly decreasing, and the sky begun to show evidences of approaching daylight.

"Start up yer hoss, Mr. Brant," said the guide. "We've got some thirty odd miles to ride afore we ken count ourselves any ways safe. We ken make it easy enough, but it stands us in hand to git ten or a dozen miles away from this afore daylight fairly breaks, and then we must take it easy, fur it won't do to git our hosses blowed. Thar's stragglin' parties of the rebils about this kentry all the time, and we may need all the wind that these four legs under us ken carry, to git us out of the way of some of the scamps."

They all pushed their horses to the gallop, and the road disappeared rapidly under their feet. To young Brant the hour, the

fresh, cool air, the spirited horse he rode, the remembrance of the great danger from which he had lately escaped, the sense of the lesser peril he was now in, and the hope of again meeting Mabel Mercer, combined to exhilarate him, and to render the ride a thing to be remembered in after life. The boy, Jake, also, was running over with excitement, and it needed frequent admonitions from Woodworth to restrain his ardent desire to get on faster. The sense of his newly-acquired freedom, and the hope of preserving it, were even stronger feelings than those which actuated the whiter and better-educated young gentleman who rode before him.

They rode thus for about an hour and a half, over a rather rough road, when the guide turned into a smaller and less frequented road, which led off to the left, and let his horse drop into a walk. Brant followed his example. It was now nearly daylight, but no signs of life had as yet been seen at any of the farm-houses or cabins they had passed. Bob thought it a good time to gain some enlightenment from his companion, and accordingly asked him how he had happened to meet him at Curwin's tavern, and on the road, after he had been captured.

The old scout chuckled:

"Oh, that was easy enough," he said. "As I told ye, I hain't been in this kentry till lately, and none of the folks livin' about here knowd me; so 'twasn't near so dangerous as it is on t'other side the Tennessee, though of course it's ruther resky like. Besides, I've got inter the way of makin' friends with the niggers, and relyin' on them considabul, and I ken tell ye that I hevn't tried one on 'em yit that was any ways onreliable, leastways, not to me. Among 'em I struck that boy, Jake, and I must say for the young nigger, that he's put me up to one or two tricks, sech as I wouldn't 'a thort on myself. I knew from Major Mercer's Pharaoh, who is a most overpowerin' sort of a nigger, and he's some onaccountabul ways of gittin' around and doin' things, when ye was to be at Curwin's tarvern, and the boy stuffed the old man up with a tale I told him to tell about me, so that I was all right on that goose question. I soon found out that two of the men who were in thar when you come in didn't hev any too much secesh into 'em; so that if it had come to a fight we'd hev had a far show, though them two critters was no 'count ornary cowards, anyhow. When young Mercer come in, I saw it was all right; for that game was as plain as the nose on my face, which is tolabul plain. I 'spect I could hev got into that yere fort, and got out of it, too, by myself; but I knowed nothin' about readin' and writin', and it needed a man of edication and discarnment, like yourself, for that work."

Brant thought of Mabel Mercer's request to him, through Charley, to leave the dangerous service on which he was employed, and the feeling that this rough and untutored backwoodsman could surpass him in the vocation he had chosen, contributed to shake his resolution to devote his life to his country as a spy and scout; but he summoned up his patriotism, and endeavored to shake off the feeling.

"Well," continued Woodworth, "sence that affair at the tarvern, I've been a-layin' around here o' nights, for I knowed ye'd git out o' the fort as soon as ye could, and knowed ye'd hev to leave at night. I had two or three niggers I could depend on, a-watchin' too, and I 'spect ye wouldn't hev gone fur without lightin' on some of us. Here, Jake!"

The black boy rode up.

"How was it old Curwin happened to be out at that time o' night? Be sure ye tell me the truth, now."

"Why, Mass' Bill, de ole man an' me, we went out to steal a pig which de ole man knowed about; but he couldn't find de pig, an' he was awful mad, an' so he drunk up all de whisky in de bottle, an' guv me a thrashin'; an' we was a-goin' home when he saw this gen'leman in the road, an' den—"

"That'll do, now, black boy, and you may fall back. As I was a-sayin', Mr. Brant, I was lyin' around, and thort I'd take a little scout up the road, and thar I saw that bloody old secesher a-marchin' you along. I dug* inter the timber till I got nigh yer, and then ye'd stopped and was a-settin' down; so I sneaked up quiet-like, till I got near enough to knock the old wretch 'over the head with the butt of my pistil. The boy saw me as I come up, but I had got him trained, and knowed he wouldn't be in the way."

"It seemed to me," said Bob, "that you did not arrive a moment too soon, for I had nearly made up my mind that I would be obliged to go back to the fort and get my nock stretched."

The conversation then turned upon the news, which Brant was anxious to learn, but of which his companion could tell him little, as he was conversant only with matters in the immediate neighborhood. He could assure Brant, however, that great preparations were making, and that an expedition would soon start out to accomplish the capture of Forts Henry and Donelson. This was joyful news to our hero, who was convinced that the fall of these strongholds would insure the evacuation of Columbus, which would be followed by the Federal occupation of Jackson.

Thus they journeyed along, at a moderate pace, beguiling the way with conversation, Woodworth relating, in his quaint and peculiar manner, some incidents of his scouting life in Missouri, Kentucky, and Tennessee, to which Brant listened with interest, though it must be confessed that his thoughts principally tended toward Mabel Mercer. Woodworth occasionally altered his direction; taking roads apparently unfrequented, which were often nothing more than bridle paths. Thus far they had only encountered two persons; one a white man, who was hauling wood out of the forest with a yoke of oxen, and who eyed them suspiciously and bid them a surly good morning; and the other a negro, whom Woodworth stopped, and whom he asked a few questions concerning the road, inquiring whether he had seen any Confederate cavalry scouting around lately. The questions concerning the roads were answered satisfactorily, but on the other point, the man either could or would give no information, further than that they were scouting the country most of the time.

It was high noon, by the sun, when the party reached a small valley, where the road, passing through a forest of immense trees, was crossed by a rivulet which was not at that season large enough to be called a brook. The guide looked up at the luminary, which was faintly visible through light clouds, and brought his horse to a halt.

"Mr. Brant," said he, "do ye feel as if ye could eat suthin'?"

"I think I could, if I had it to eat. You do not expect to find any thing about here, do you?"

"Well, ye see, I'm sorter like an army, and when I move inter the enemy's kentry, I ginerally hev my supply stations, as they call 'em, some'res about, and 'pears to me I've got a *cache* around here. Yes, thar's the gum tree, broke off at the top. Follow me."

Woodworth turned into the timber, and followed the course of the rivulet for a few rods, when he stopped and tied his horse to a tree, his example being imitated by his companions. After looking around a moment or two, he went to a flat stone, which he lifted up, and discovered a hollow scooped out beneath it, from which he produced some cold boiled salt pork and some crackers, wrapped up in a cloth.

"I hid that yere," said he, "when I come along this road the last time, fur I knowed it would stand me in good hand ef the varmints didn't get at it. But nothin' hes tetched it, so fur's I see. Help yerself, Mr. Brant."

Cutting off a fair slice, or chunk, of the pork, he gave it to Jake, with some crackers, and bade him keep at a respectful distance, for this "poor white" had a high idea of his dignity as a white man, and thought it beneath him to eat with a "nigger."

The two scouts then fell to in good earnest, with knives, fingers, and teeth, and soon exhausted the contents of this forest larder, after which, they quenched their thirst at the rivulet, mounted their horses, and proceeded on their way, feeling much refreshed by their rude repast.

CHAPTER XVI.

A Race and its Result.

THE party rode on, without meeting with any molestation, until it was near sunset. They got on rapidly, as their horses were still in excellent condition, but as they were now in the turnpike, Woodworth proceeded more carefully, and at every cross-road took the precaution of sending Jake ahead to reconnoiter. That youth understood the duty with a high sense of the responsibility resting upon him, and flourished old Curwin's pistol in a manner that threatened danger to himself or his companions. Woodworth was obliged to tell him to put the pistol away, or he would take it from him.

The road led again through a thick wood, at the opening of which there appeared to be a lane tending to the right. Jake was sent ahead, as usual, to reconnoiter. The boy stopped his horse at the opening of the lane, peered down it a moment, and then galloped back, with eyes wide open and mouth agape.

"Massa Bill," exclaimed the excited darkey. "I seed 'em. Dar they is, down dat road, on hosses, with soger coats, and guns."

"Federate cavalry scouts, of course," said old Bill, calmly. How fur down the road, Jake?"

"Oh, a good ways, and only a-walkin' ther hosses."

"Let's ride along slowly, Mr. Brant," said the old man, " so's they shan't suspicion us, and then if they hail us, we'll hev to run fur it. 'Twon't be long afore we ken git whar we'll be tollabul safe."

The three then rode along at a gentle trot, Jake keeping well to the left, and Woodworth forming the right flank. As they reached the road, old Bill cast his eye down it, and plainly saw seven or eight cavalrymen, in the Confederate uniform, at a less distance than Jake had given him to suppose. They spied our three travelers at the same instant, and spurred their horses.

"Who goes there? Halt!" rung out on the air.

"Ride now, Mr. Brant, fur yer life," said Woodworth, as he urged his horse forward.

Brant struck his spurs into his horse, and the animal started forward with a bound. Jake was already quite a distance ahead, and Woodworth followed rapidly. Several shots were fired by the Confederates, but none of them took effect upon the party. As they had used their horses carefully, and kept them in fair condition, they made good time, and easily run away from the jaded animals of their pursuers, who, after a run of a mile, gave up the chase in despair

Woodworth and Brant pulled up their panting animals to a walk, and the old man ordered Jake to moderate his speed and ride close to them.

"Well out of that scrape, Mr. Brant," said old Bill. "Inside of an hour we'll be as safe as we ken be in this yere kentry."

The words were hardly out of his mouth, when the old scout espied a fresh danger. As they emerged from the wood, a wide cornfield spread out to the right, and across it was coming a body of horsemen. They were evidently Confederate cavalry, and were spurring their horses over the rough ground, as if they wished to head off the little party.

Again it was ride for life, and the two scouts followed Jake, who was kicking his heels against the sides of his saddleless and bridleless horse, and urging him furiously forward. Their horses had got their breath again, and the road was level and smooth; but their enemies were too near for them to escape scatheless. They had almost passed the cornfield, and were about to enter the wood again, when the Confederates halted and fired a volley. Brant saw the dust fly from Woodworth's saddle, and at the same instant felt a sharp pang in his right arm, as if a hot iron had been suddenly run through it. But he only urged on his horse the more, and as the Confederates were obliged to stop to take down a portion of the fence, the little party soon distanced them. Then Bob began to feel faint.

"Woodworth," said he, "I am hit."

"Stop yer hoss. Hi! Jake, halt there! Good God! Mr. Brant, yer bleedin' like a bull. What a quantity of blood thar is in young veins, for sartin'! Give me yer handkercher, fur that blood has got to be stopped."

Brant handed him the handkerchief, and the old man, without dismounting, quickly cut the sleeve from the wounded arm, and pressed his thumbs and fingers hurriedly and roughly around the bullet-hole.

"It hain't touched the bone, Mr. Brant, and ye'll soon git over it. Let me jest stop that bleedin', and we must be off."

The old scout then tied the handkerchief around the arm of the younger one, pulling it so tightly that the pain made him wince and contract his brows; but he strove to suppress any indication of suffering, as he looked over his shoulder and saw the Confederates coming on behind them, at no great distance.

Again they spurred their horses, and again they distanced their pursuers. Thus they rode on for nearly half an hour, when they came in sight of a small hut, which looked like a negro cabin, situated in a clearing at the end of a turn in the road.

"Halt here, Mr. Brant," said Woodworth. "Git off yer hoss, and run into that cabin. Don't stop to ask questions. It's all right. Here, take yer pistils."

The old man then handed Brant the pistols from his own holsters, placing them in his left hand, and rode off without another word of explanation, leading the riderless horse. Bob did not stop to wonder or to think. Death or capture was behind him, and in the cabin was his only chance of safety; besides, he had unlimited confidence in Woodworth, and the old scout had assured him that it was "all right." So he stepped quietly to the door and entered.

"Massa Brant!"

"What, old Pharaoh? Pharaoh, I am wounded, and am pursued. Can you hide me?"

"'Spect I ken, Massa Brant. Thar ain't no time for talkin', is there?"

"No, old man; they will be here in a few minutes."

A hasty glance showed Brant that the little cabin had but one room, one side of which was almost entirely occupied by a broad fire-place. On another side was a rickety bedstead, covered with some tattered quilts. A rough table, a bench, a broken chair, and a few iron pots and skillets, appeared to complete the regular furniture of the habitation; but at this time the room was nearly filled with a litter of household articles, boxes, bags and bedding, which were scattered around confusedly, and which evidently did not belong there. In a corner, between the fire-place and the bedstead, was a pile of old clothes, empty bags, sheets, blankets, coverlets, and odds and ends, which reached nearly up to the roof. Old Pharaoh went to this pile, pulled it down, and placed two empty boxes on end against the sides of the cabin.

"Git in thar, Massa Brant," said he, "'tween dem boxes, and I'll kiver ye up keerfully, so's you ken git yer breff, and you'll lie as snug as a coon in a holler log."

Bob accordingly sat down in the corner, still holding his pistols in his left hand, and the old negro piled the quilts and other articles over him thickly and loosely, but was careful to leave him a breathing place by the side of one of the boxes.

He was not a moment too soon, for the hiding place was hardly finished when the sound of horses' feet, advancing rapidly, were heard, and they stopped in front of the cabin. Directly the door was opened so violently as almost to upset old Pharaoh, and a man, in the uniform of a Confederate officer, entered, followed by four of his men, all armed with rifles, shot-guns, pistols and knives.

"Hallo, uncle!" said the leader. "Have you seen two men and a little nigger riding by here lately?"

"Yes, massa officer. 'Pears like it wasn't more'n ten minutes ago. Thar was an old man and a young one, and a little nigger on a hoss with nothin' but a halter. They stopped out in the road a minute or two, 'cause one of em had his arm tied up, and 'peared to feel kinder faint. When they rode off again, the old man was leadin' the young one's hoss."

"Those are the men we are after. Martin, does the road look as if the horses had stopped there?"

"Yes, sir; but they have all gone on again, as there are tracks of three horses beyond."

"Then the old darkey has told us the truth."

"O yes, massa officer; it's Goramighty's troof what I tole you. But their hosses 'peared to be mighty tired, and, if you've got good hosses, you mought ketch 'em."

"The fact is, our horses are worse off than theirs. These men," he continued, addressing one of his companions, "would have been worth a pretty pile to us, dead or alive, if we could have caught them, for I think one of them was old Woodworth, that infernal Yankee scout we have heard of, and the other must have been that young chap who got out of Donelson last night, a deserter or a spy—no one seemed to be certain which. But our horses are all knocked up, and there is no use in trying to follow them any nearer the Yankee lines. Who do you belong to, uncle, and what are you doing here?"

"Me, massa? I b'longs to Major Mercer, what's been livin' down to Jackson; but he's gwine to move up yere now. His house is nigh about a mile from yere, and these is some of the niggers' things."

"Is there any one at the house? Could we get any thing to eat there, and some fodder for our horses?"

"Goramighty, no, massa! Thar ain't nobody up to the house, 'cept two or three niggers, and they hain't got nuffin for tharselves to eat, scacely, and won't have nuffin, till the things comes up from Tennessee."

"Well, we must go hungry, then, for I see you have nothing here. Your master is a loyal man, I suppose?"

"Does that mean a 'Federate? Oh, yis, he's jest one o' the best kind o' 'Federates, and allus was."

"He will have to be careful how he acts around here, for the Yankees are getting into this part of the country, and their scouts are growing too plenty about here. But it will not be long before we will drive every one of the infernal thieves out of the State. Come, boys, let us be getting off and hunting for something to eat."

"Hold on a bit, Cap'n," said one of the men. "The nights are gettin' cold, and a blanket is a good thing to have. I've got my eye on one over thar in the corner, which I reckon I'll confisticate."

As he spoke, he moved toward the pile which covered Brant.

"None o' that, now, mister soger!" exclaimed old Pharaoh, who had watched the movement. "Them blankets ain't none o' your'n, and Massa Charley will be mighty mad ef they're tetched, 'cause he's gwine to jine the cavalry, and says he wants all he kin git, to warm his own men."

The man did not heed the remonstrance, but pulled a blanket from the pile. Pharaoh trembled with fear lest the hiding-place of Brant would be discovered, but strove to conceal his anxiety, contenting himself with muttering and grumbling, threatening the soldier with the wrath of "Massa Charley." It happened that the best blanket of the pile, that which the man coveted, lay loosely on the top, and, as he picked it off, there was nothing discovered beneath. If Brant knew that it was being taken, he was entitled to credit for great steadiness of nerve, for the slightest movement would have stirred his covering and induced suspicion.

"You ken tell your Massa Charley," said the Confederate, as he deliberately rolled up the blanket, "that he ken hev this back when he gits his men into the service. It mought as well be mustered in now as at any other time."

The officer and his men then left the house, mounted their horses, and the whole party returned by the road over which they had pursued Brant and his friend.

"Gorry!" ejaculated old Pharaoh, as he watched their receding forms, dimly seen in the growing dusk. "Ain't I mighty glad they's gone, though? They give this old nigger an orful scare. Cuss 'em, anybody's nigger's a white man alongside o' them froat-cutters."

He watched them until they were out of sight, and then called to Brant:

"Come out, now, Massa Brant. They's all gone."

Hearing no answer, he stepped to the pile, muttering:

"'Spect I done forgot he's got a lame arm, and can't git hisself out."

Hastily tearing down the pile of cotton and woolen, he saw Brant sitting as if asleep, with his head dropped upon his breast. The pain of his wound and the tightness of the bandage, combined with the lack of air, had caused him to faint.

CHAPTER XVII.

In Comfortable Quarters.

"Oh, Goramighty!" exclaimed the old negro, "he's gone dead. No, he ain't he's only swounded away. I jest wish Missy Mercer was here, or Aunt Jule, or somebody."

Fortunately, Pharaoh did not confine himself to lamentations, but drew the young man out from his uncomfortable place of concealment, and set him up on some blankets against the side of the house. Then he ran for some water, which he speedily brought, and dashed it liberally in Brant's face. As this remedy was not effectual at the instant, he thrust a quantity of snuff in the nose of the insensible man, when his efforts were rewarded by a slight sneeze, and Brant opened his eyes, slowly, at first, and then stared wildly about the little room.

"Look up, Massa Brant; don't ye be scar'd, for I's old Pharaoh, and yer safe now. Those 'Federate froat-cutters are all done gone."

"My arm—it pains me—it feels dead. Give me some water."

A drink revived the young man, and then Pharaoh took the wounded arm tenderly in his black and rough paws, and one or two tears dropped upon it.

"None of your salt water, old man," said Bob, who had now fully recovered his senses. "Light a candle, or something, and come and untie this bandage."

Pharaoh hastened to strike a light, and then carefully untied the bandage, above which the arm was badly swollen. It was only a flesh wound, but the ball had cut a large vein, and the loss of blood had been considerable. The old negro muttered plaintively as he washed the wound.

"It's gone right through this poor arm, but it hain't touched no bone, Massa Brant, and it's a nice clean hole, and that's a good thing. Oh, it hurts this ole nigger mighty bad, to think how many good men a-fightin' fur freedom will hev wuss holes'n this bored through 'em. But them what does it, Goramighty knows they'll hev to pay sharp for what they're a-doin agin his laws. Now, I've got some sarve, real nice sarve, that ole Aunt Jule made herself, and it's jest the 'mazinest best thing that ever was, fur cuts and burns and bruises; and I'll jest put some of that on yer arm."

"Be quick about it, then, and talk less."

Bob Brant was evidently peevish and impatient, and old Pharaoh, thus admonished, hastened to find his salve, and soon bound up the wound comfortably, though not after the manner of regular surgeons. He then made a sling of Brant's handkerchief, with which he tied up the arm in an easy position, and stepped back to survey his work.

"There, Massa Brant, jest you sit there quiet like, while I run up to the house and tell Miss Mabel, and fetch somethin' you ken eat."

"Tell who?"

"Tell Miss Mabel—Massa Mercer's Mabel, you know. Didn't you hear me tell them 'Federates that Major Mercer was a-movin' up yere?"

"No; I heard nothing you said, after the first few words. But if Mabel Mercer is near here, hurry on, old man, for God's sake. You must not ask her to come here to-night. But perhaps Mr. Charles can come."

"Oh no; Massa Charley ain't here now. Thar's nobody up to the house 'ceptin' Miss Mabel and Missy Mercer, and some o' de cullud folks. I don't 'spect either of 'em ken come to-night, as they's all tumbled up. Now jest you keep still, and I'll be back mighty quick."

As the old man hurried off, Bob Brant reflected upon his condition, and saw no reason to complain. He had a wounded arm, but that was nothing to a strong and healthy young man. He had got well out of his scrape at Curwin's tavern; he had safely escaped from the rebel stronghold on the Tennessee; he had been rescued, at the nick of time, from the clutches of Curwin; his papers were safe in the possession of Woodworth, and were on their way to a place where their value would be appreciated; and, above all, here he was, almost within reach of Mabel Mercer. Under the circumstances, the wounded arm was a positive blessing, and he inwardly thanked the Confederate who had fired the bullet. He soon came to the conclusion that the wound would get well slowly; that it was more severe than he had thought, and he was sure that it would require very careful nursing. The truth is, that the young man was too much weakened by want of sleep and food, by his long ride, and by pain and loss of blood, to form any more high-minded, patriotic and severe resolutions, or even to remember those which he had previously formed. He felt an agreeable lassitude, mingled with pleasant anticipation, and was ready to accept, thankfully, any blessings that Providence might have in store for him, without giving himself unnecessary trouble about labor and duty. He then begun to think of the possibility of Mabel Mercer making her appearance there, in that cabin, perhaps that night, and then—alas for his character as a patriot and a hero!—he actually thought of the sorry figure he would present to her, with his cut coat-sleeve, his disordered and bloody clothes, his tangled hair, and his general air of slouchiness. He rose with difficulty, endeavored to smooth his rough hair and arrange his attire so as to make himself partially presentable, and then tottered to the broken chair which he had placed in a corner, and braced himself up, vainly striving to appear easy and non-chalant.

He had hardly seated himself, when the door opened, and in stepped Mabel Mercer herself, followed by Pharaoh and a negro woman, both loaded down with sheets, pillows, eatables and other articles. Brant attempted to rise, but his previous efforts had exhausted him, and he sunk back upon the chair.

"Miss Mercer, this is too much honor."

"No honor at all, if you please ; and if it was, no honor could be too great for a brave man who has been wounded in the cause of his country. Now, you are not to say another word, but just obey Aunt Jule and me, and wait as patiently as possible until we make you as comfortable as we can. Pharaoh, put down those things, and don't stand there staring. Then start a fire, and try to make this place look a little decent."

Brant's eyes followed her graceful form wonderingly and wistfully, as she moved lightly and airily around the small room. In a very short time, with the assistance of the old negress, who seemed to know just what to do, and just how to do it, she had made a great change in the cabin, and it really looked comfortable and cheerful. A bright fire blazed upon the hearth, over which a kettle was soon singing merrily, and the fair Mabel was on her knees before the fire, toasting thin slices of bread, with a fork so short that Bob was unhappy for fear that her delicate hands would be scorched. A good couch of blankets was made upon the rickety bedstead, on which pillows were placed and sheets were spread, and Brant, with the assistance of old Pharaoh and the

negress, was laid upon it unresistingly. And then he was propped up with pillows and quilts, so that he could see the fire and the busy Mabel, and the bright face of Pharaoh ; and then Aunt Jule, softly soothing the wounded arm, and calling him "Honey," washed it in nice, warm water, abused Pharaoh for his clumsiness, and called for more of her wonderful "sarve ;" and then Mabel, with her face all ablaze, had to leave her toast-making to find some linen and lint, and had to stop as she brought it, to take a shy peep at the fair, white arm, and to tell Aunt Jule to be very careful not to hurt it—a suggestion which that female treated quite scornfully—and, in short, Bob Brant was in elysium, and thought that it was a very pleasant thing to be wounded.

"Laws a-massy, Miss Mabel," said Aunt Jule, as she re-slung Brant's arm in a clean and soft handkerchief, and laid it across his breast, "you've been and made toast enough for a reg'ment. Jest you fix that tea now, while I look arter the jelly. I don't 'low nobody to touch my jellys, 'cept sickness or death."

Mabel started up, as if aroused from a reverie, bustled about, drew the tea in a dainty little tea-pot, poured it out in a shining cup, and placed it upon a waiter before our hero, together with the hot buttered toast, and a plentiful supply of Aunt Jule's jelly, which was only less wonderful than her "sarve." Then she drew the broken chair to the bedside, and actually insisted upon feeding that rough fellow with her own fair hands. Our hero was quite overcome, and a few drops of moisture which stole from his eyes proved his lack of the proper heroic qualities. But he had no mother, and all this was new to him.

"Does your arm pain you so much ?"

"Oh, no, scarcely any, thanks to you and Aunt Jule. But it is so sweet to be wounded, when I can be here, and with you !"

He felt that there was a wound in his heart, which could not be healed so easily as that in his arm.

Mabel concealed her blushes by pouring out some more tea.

Brant drank his tea and munched his toast slowly, for he wished to prolong his pleasure. Mabel was anxious to know his adventures after he parted with her brother, for Charley had given her a vivid description of the scene at Curwin's tavern, and of his triumphant entry into the fort. As Bob related his several escapes, she listened eagerly, with little ladylike ejaculations of wonder, pity, and fear. It was somewhat like the old story of Othello and Desdemona.

Brant then inquired about Major Mercer and the rest of his family, and was informed that they were engaged in the unpleasant labor of moving, but would soon be settled down again.

"You can not imagine," said Mabel, "what a change has come over father. He is nothing like he used to be. He had a great deal of trouble with the authorities at Jackson, when they learned that he intended to leave, and they run off two or three of his best negroes. He expects to be obliged to leave behind much of what belongs to him in Jackson, but his money is safe in Louisville, and that is a great comfort to him. The house we are to live in here is a small house, compared with that at Jackson, and it is not a nice one, but we will be much happier than among the rebel officers and soldiers, and mamma is very much pleased. The house belongs to ma's brother William, who's a good Union man and loves us all dearly. Father is a good Union man, too, at last, and abuses the secessionists like a man, when he is away from Jackson. And that's all, I believe."

"Come now, Miss Mabel," broke in Aunt Jule. "Jest stop that talkin', and let the young gen'l'man alone, and come right home 'long with me; fur Miss Car'line 'll be oneasy."

"Wait a moment, Jake, Pharaoh says he thinks those rebels will not be back here tonight, Mr. Brant, and I am sure of it; so you must sleep soundly and feel fresh in the morning. I will be here early, and Charley will be home to-morrow, and then we will take you up to the house. Good night, and pleasant dreams to you!"

Mabel Mercer tripped away, carrying Bob Brant's sunshine with her; but she left him a warmth about the heart that was very pleasant to him. He prepared himself to enjoy a good night's rest. Bidding Pharaoh to bring him his pistols, he examined them, and laid one within reach of his well arm, giving the other to the old negro. Pharaoh rolled himself up in a blanket, and laid down in front of the door. Even the thought of Mabel Mercer could not keep Brant awake, and he soon dropped into a doze.

Pharaoh had hardly commenced to snore,

when his slumber was interrupted by a gentle tapping at the door of the cabin.

"Who's thar?" said the old negro, softly, as he sat up in his blanket.

"It's me—it's Jake."

"Who's Jake?"

"Is Massa Brant in thar? He knows me."

"What is it, Pharaoh?" asked Bob, half awakened.

"Some nigger boy, I 'spect—says his name's Jake, and you knows him."

"Let him in. What do you want here, you ebony imp? What is the matter now?"

"Massa Bill tole me to come back yere, sah. He tole me I b'longs to you now, an' I must see how you's gittin' on."

"Very well. I can not say that I am obliged to him, as I fear you will prove rather troublesome property. Are you hungry?"

"No, sah."

"Pharaoh, give him a blanket, and let him curl up somewhere. Go to sleep, imp, and dream of the promised land."

The "imp" showed his ivories until, as some old poet says, they almost "made a sunshine in a shady place," and dropped in a corner. Pharaoh grumbled a little, and snored again. Brant was soon immersed in dreams, in which Mabel Mercer was strangely mixed up with prisons and grinning Africans.

CHAPTER XVIII.

Major Mercer's Policy.

THE first thing the boy Jake did, upon awakening in the morning, was to ask for some blacking and a brush, with which to polish the boots of his new master; the first thing old Pharaoh did, was to scold the said boy Jake for disturbing the slumbers of the said master; and the first thing Bob Brant did, was to call for hot water and soap and a towel, that he might clean the outward man. Those necessaries were not to be had in a moment, however, and when our hero had succeeded in working himself up to an unpleasant condition of peevishness, he was astonished by the entrance of Charley Mercer, who brought sunshine with him, and drove the clouds from the faces of all three.

"What in creation is the matter with you all?" exclaimed the hearty young fellow, as he gazed upon their grim faces. "Why, Brant, you look like a thunder cloud, and Pharaoh is solemn as an owl, and who is this young darkey?"

"We didn't 'spect you so soon, Massa Charley," said old Pharaoh. "As fur that young nigger, I dunno whar he cum from, but I don't b'lieve thar's much good in him, nohow. He's jest been botherin' the life out o' me, for a boot brush and some blackin', to do Massa Brant's boots, jest's ef he knowed how, when his olders an' his betters is here, too."

"Well, never mind the boy. Let me see you look a little more cheerful. Here, Mr. Brant, I have brought you some clothes to wear, and you must hurry and put on something clean and nice, as sister Mabel will be here shortly."

This announcement brought Bob to his feet instantly, and with the assistance of Charley Mercer and old Pharaoh, he was soon made clean and presentable. But the change in his personal appearance was not made any too soon, for Mabel directly entered, bright and cheery as ever, and then there was a happy party in the little cabin. The boy Jake obtained the privilege of blacking Bob's boots all he chose, and polished them until they were even blacker and more shining than his own ebony face.

Mabel anxiously inquired of Bob Brant whether he thought he could bear the journey to the house, and whether he could possibly walk half a mile; and that young hypocrite replied that he thought he could, if he had a stick or something to lean on; when the young lady offered her arm, which he instantly accepted. And as they marched to Major Mercer's new residence, which was a small one story farm-house, but with comfortable negro quarters. Pharaoh wished the boy Jake to remain with him, as he thought the young African needed his personal supervision; but the boy said that Massa Bill had told him to stick to Massa Brant, and he meant to do it; so, at the solicitation of our hero, he was allowed to accompany them, and was thereafter installed as his special body servant.

They found Mrs. Mercer at the house, who welcomed Brant very kindly, showed him the little room which she had fitted up for him, and soon made him perfectly at home. Major Mercer arrived after a few days, bringing up the rear, with all of his property that he had been permitted to bring away from Jackson, from which place he

had been glad to escape with his life and liberty.

Those were happy days that Bob Brant passed at the little farm-house. He had never been any half as happy before, and had never thought that life could have so many charms for him. He did not pass his time in "making love," for he found it ready-made to his hand, but in loving and being loved, and in wondering how long such happiness could last. His arm speedily healed, so that he could easily have dispensed with his sling; but he did not do so, as it was so sweet to be wounded there, and so pleasant to be nursed by Mrs. Mercer — and Mabel. The young man had changed under the enervating influence of this first affection. He was no longer anxious to rush on and sacrifice his life for his country, but absolutely dreaded the time when, what he still considered his duty, should again call him into active service. The change might be pitiable, but the happiness was enviable.

As for Major Mercer, he sat down quietly, and waited for the storm of war to blow over him. He now hated secession and all secessionists, but much of his natural timidity remained, and he was by no means an outspoken partisan. He had lost much, and feared that he might lose much more; but he was now quite determined to lose it; if it must be lost, on the side of the Union. Thus far he was willing to go, no further. He was a Union man, but conservative—of himself and his property.

"Wife," he said, one evening, as the family, including Brant, were collected together, "this is pleasant, far more so than at Jackson, and we have much to be thankful for."

"It is liberty, husband; it is freedom from the scoundrels, swindlers, and traitors who are striving to destroy the Union and the peace of every fireside in it. But we will be much happier when we can see the flag of the Union flying over our house. For my part, I would like to raise it this very day."

"Mother and I are making one," whispered Mabel to Bob, and she was rewarded for the information by a pressure of the hand.

"It may be as you say," answered Major Mercer; "but it is not well to compromise ourselves too far at present. The truth should not be told at all times. As for a flag, don't talk of raising one yet. It is a great deal to be thankful for, that we are unmolested here, and are likely to be so."

"Don't be too sure of that, father," broke in Charley Mercer. The rebel guerillas have lately been getting thicker in this part of the country, and parties of them have been within a few miles of our house. If you will give me your permission, I will conceal all the arms we happen to have, so that they can not be found if the guerillas should make us a visit."

"You see, wife," said the Major, "Charles coincides with me. I told you that we must be careful. By all means, Charles, conceal the arms, as we would be unable to use them in our defense."

"I can fight, father," said Charley Mercer.

"So can I," said Brant.

"So can I," said Mabel, with a right royal flash of the eye.

"So can even old Pharaoh," said Mrs. Mercer, quietly but confidently.

"What, wife!" exclaimed the Major, starting up with his countenance flushed with anger and astonishment. "Would you ask our niggers to fight for us? The cowards would run at the first flash of a musket. Besides, what defense have we, but our own arms?"

"If you please, father," said Charley, "I, Major-General Charles Mercer, with the assistance of Lieutenant-Colonel Brant, chief of artillery, have fortified the smoke-house, so that it will stand a siege against any thing but artillery."

"Charles! Charles! this is no child's play. You talk boyishly and recklessly. Let me hear no more of such nonsense. But you had better conceal the arms, as you said. I have no fear that the guerillas will offer any serious molestation. But their presence might probably be uncomfortable to our friend, Mr. Brant, and perhaps it would be better for him to find some temporary place of concealment."

"I will manage that, father."

Thereafter, Charley Mercer and old Pharaoh constituted themselves scouts for that outpost, as they called the house and its appurtenances, and scoured the adjoining country thoroughly, watching for indications of guerillas in the neighborhood. The boy Jake was on the scout also, and his habits and instinct enabled him to gain intelligence with more ease and certainty than his older and more prudent companions. One morning early, as Charley Mercer and Pharaoh were just issuing out, they met the boy running toward them, with eyes wide open and mouth agape, and panting with the exertions he had made.

"Massa Charles, dey's comin'! dey's comin'! I seed 'em myself — a whole squadroon o' dem rebel fellers, on ther hosses, an' lookin' jest like I used to see 'em around ole Massa Curwin's."

"Pharaoh," said Charles, "run to the house and tell Mr. Brant to get ready to hide."

"Now Massa Charley, don't you go to b'lieve a word that scrumptious little nigger says. He's seen a stump, an' it's dun scar'd him outer his wits, ef he ever had any. I ken see in his eye he's a lyin' at this minute. That stock o' niggers is allus skeary, an' apt to be terrible onsartin."

"Run to the house, Pharaoh, and do as I told you."

The old negro went off grumbling, and young Mercer questioned the boy, and soon saw reason to believe that his tale was true, although it might be somewhat exaggerated. He accordingly hastened to the house, and conveyed Brant to the place of concealment which had been prepared for him, in one of the negro quarters, and bade him lie quiet while he went back to the house and reconnoitered. The boy Jake showed more prudence than Pharaoh would have been willing to give him credit for, by also going into hiding.

Brant waited nearly two hours for his friend, seeing nothing and hearing nothing, and his anxiety made the time seem longer, and made his confinement irksome to him. At last, when Charley Mercer came, his eyes sparkled with fire, and his sides shook with laughter.

"Brant, my boy, it's the best thing! The best thing you ever saw! The best thing of the season or any other season! The best thing that could possibly have happened, for all of us, as sure as I am a sinner!"

"What's the matter? Nobody hurt, I judge from your countenance."

"Yes, somebody hurt, awfully hurt, in feelings, and that is no less a man than my father, Major Mercer. You know how father has always been, how off-and-onish, how timid and non-committal. If he had not been my father, I could not have respected him, and hardly did, at that. Well, the rebels did not respect his neutrality, either—not a bit. They took what they chose, and stormed about the house as they pleased; but that was nothing—they actually kicked him—kicked Major Mercer, the representative of one of the best familes in West Tennessee and Kentucky—kicked him, and slapped his face, first on the Union side, and then on the rebel side. Oh, how it roused him! He cursed them, and told them that they would suffer for that indignity; but they laughed at him and rode away. Isn't it glorious?"

"Charley, I really do not see how you can laugh when your father has been insulted and abused."

"It does seem hard, but I am glad of it, for he is a thorough Union man now, without any ifs or ands. He will never go back, either, but will fight them now to the death, I will bet my life. He is raging around the house in a terrible fury. Let us go up and see him. He does not know that I witnessed the kicking and slapping."

"I hope they did not offer to insult Mabel."

"Not at all. She was in her room, and they merely looked in to see that no one else was there, and left her in peace. Mother simply looked on and said nothing, and was not molested. Father's misfortune happened in front of the house, where he was endeavoring to 'explain his position' to the rebels. They were not real guerillas."

The friends then walked into the house.

CHAPTER XIX.

The Impromptu Fortress.

WHEN Brant and young Mercer entered the house, they found Major Mercer in the parlor with his wife and Mabel. Mrs. Mercer looked indignant, but calm and composed. Mabel's face was flushed, and her eyes were flashing. The Major himself was walking, excitedly, up and down the room, speaking incoherently, and, it must be confessed, with occasional profanity.

Charley asked, quite coolly:

"What is the matter, father?"

"Matter! Matter enough, and too much. Would you believe it, my son, those rebel rascals have actually dared—have had the audacity and the insolence—to kick me, yes, *me*, the representative of the old Mercer stock—a stock that has never been dishonored, since Kentucky was a State. Yes, they kicked me, Charles, and slapped me in the face. Curse them, if I had had a pistol, or a knife, they would have learned what it is to insult Henry Mercer."

"I hope you had not been so rash as to tell them you were a Unionist."

"No; I wish I had, and then I might have excused them. I was endeavoring to explain to them the delicate position in which I found myself, telling them that my interests lay with the South, but I was situated near the North, and much of my property was there, and I thought it was only fair that I should be allowed to preserve my neutrality, and I only asked to be let alone in peace. Then their leader spoke up: 'Oh, bah!' said he, 'you are neither fish nor flesh, but a big bloated bullfrog. You are with us to save your niggers, and with the Lincolnites to keep your land.' And then—"

"Did you believe him, father?"

"Charles?"

"Did you believe him, father?"

"What do you mean?"

"Did you believe the man when he said that?"

The Major cooled down immediately, and, for a few moments, was lost in thought.

"My son," said he, "in the excitement of the moment I suppose I thought nothing about believing or disbelieving; but when I reflect upon it, I incline to confess that he spoke the truth, or near it—nearer than I did, certainly. But I never will be guilty of making such an explanation to any of them again. I will tell them plainly that I am—as from this moment I will be—a Union man, sound and true; and then if they take me, I will do my best that they shall not take me alive."

"Father, I never honored you as much as I do at this moment."

"Caroline," continued the Major, taking his wife by both her hands, "are you willing that I take this step, and that I sacrifice every thing—slaves, lands, home, money, and life, if need be—in the cause of the Union?"

"I am, Henry. I am willing to give up every thing, and I trust that you may never change."

"Then from this day forward I will serve that cause to the extent of my ability, with my tongue, my pen, my means, and my sword, if I can. I see the error of my way. I have halted long between the wrong and the right, but now that I have taken the step, you shall never have occasion to accuse me of turning back."

"God bless you, my husband!"

"God bless you, father!"

Mabel Mercer stepped up and kissed her father's hand, and glided out of the door, followed by Brant.

"I am glad, Robert," said she, "that you did not witness what happened to father."

"So am I; but I am also glad that I did witness what has happened to him just now."

"Well, it is better to be kicked and slapped into being a Union man, than not to be one at all."

"Much better; but we will not tell him so."

"Oh, no!"

When they had talked a few moments, Major Mercer came out, accompanied by Charley. The Major was looking unusually bright and cheerful, and stepped more freely, as if he had thrown off a great load.

"Lieutenant-Colonel Brant," said he, "I understand from this young Major-General Mercer that you are acting as his Chief of Artillery and Engineers, and I desire to ask permission to visit your fortifications."

"Certainly, sir, and we are prepared to deliver up to you the command of the garrison, in virtue of your rank."

The three then proceeded to inspect the smoke-house.

"This smoke-house, as it was called, stood about one hundred yards from the dwelling-house, and was a stout log building, some twenty feet square, or more. It was a smoke-house only in name, as it had never been used for that purpose, but principally for storing. It had a large and deep cellar, which in winter commonly contained the vegetable supplies of the family. There was a small addition at one end, which covered the door. There was but one small window, with a wooden shutter. Brant and young Mercer had carefully loopholed the building for musketry, and had made ample arrangements for ventilation just under the roof, and near the floor. They had also strengthened the window-shutter and the door by thicknesses of planking. Thus the building was in an admirable condition for defense, being impervious to musket or rifle bullets, and was available for a siege against any thing but artillery.

Major Mercer surveyed the arrangements with the eye of a connoisseur, and expressed himself highly satisfied.

"Well, young gentlemen, I must confess that I do not at present see how your fortification can be improved upon. You have certainly arranged every thing as I should wish to have it arranged. It puzzles me how you can have done all this without my knowledge."

"Nothing easier, father, as you never came near here."

"Ah! I suppose so. All we can ask in addition to our means of defense would be plenty of provisions and ammunition, and some more men."

"We have plenty of men, father. There is old Pharaoh; I know he can shoot well; and so can Harry and Pete, for I have often had them out hunting with me."

"What, my son, shall we rely upon our niggers to fight for us?"

"Certainly, sir, if they are able and willing to do it."

"To be sure, my boy. I had forgotten. They are surely good enough to fight against rebels, and for their homes. I would be glad to have one of them shoot the man who kicked me, though I would rather do it myself. In what condition is the ordnance department?"

"Not first-rate. We have two rifles and a shot-gun, that I know of, and Mr. Brant and I have each two revolvers. We have run plenty of bullets, and have, I think, a fair supply of powder."

"Indeed! I must give you credit for meaning war in earnest. Wait a moment, or rather come to the house, and let me show you something."

Hastening into the house, the Major brought out a fine mahogany case, which, on being opened, disclosed a fine, short-barrelled, German rifle, in parts, with all its appurtenances complete, and in excellent condition.

"There, young gentlemen," said the Major, putting it together, and eyeing it lovingly, "is as sweet a piece as either of you ever saw, I suppose. I bought it for hunting bears in Arkansas. I don't remember how far off it will kill a bear, but it is a great distance. Let me see what my eyesight is good for now."

He then carefully loaded the piece, pointed out a bird sitting upon a limb, at such a distance that good eyes were needed to see it, took a deliberate aim, and fired. The bark flew from the limb near where the bird stood.

"Oh!" said the Major, "I am not what

I used to be, but that little bird is not a man."

"You'll do, father!" exclaimed Charley, clapping his parent on the shoulder. "And now, if you will attend to provisioning the fortress, we will see what else there is to be done."

"There is one thing forgotten, young gentlemen. You have no colors."

"Haven't we, though? Ask Mabel."

The next day Bob Brant was surprised by the appearance of old Bill Woodworth, who brought two fine breech-loading rifles.

"Thar, Mr. Brant," said the old scout; "one o' them is fur you, an' t'other is fur yer friend. They say in the camps that they're mighty nice shootin'-irons, but fur my part I don't want to be troubled with none o' them new-fangled tricks. I stick to my old long barrel, an' I ken pull down c'en a'most anythin' with her. The boy Jake—do you know that's turnin' out to be a wunnerful peart little nigger?—hunted me out and told me what you was a-contrivin' yere, an' I 'lowed I'd look in on yer. So I got permish'n, and was give these yere tools to bring you. I ken jest tell ye, Mr. Brant, that somebody ye knows on is mighty tickled about the work ye done up thar to Donelson, an' hoped yer wound wouldn't be bad. I 'lowed thar was somethin' up yere that hurted ye wuss'n that, but didn't let on. Now, good-by, an' mind to keep a sharp look-out for them guerilla thieves. This kentry's mighty hot with 'em jest now, but it won't be many days afore they're all cl'ared out," sure's I'm livin' an' a white man. Hold up, now; if I ain't a forgittin'."

The old man then unloaded from his capacious pockets a quantity of cartridges, and some canisters of rifle-powder.

"Thar, then. Part on 'em is cartridges, an' the rest is powder, and as you onderstand that sort o' guns, Mr. Brant, you ken make more cartridges. Now, I'm off."

Refusing young Mercer's pressing invitation to stop and take a "a bite and a sup," the honest old scout "loped" off, his long legs getting over the ground more rapidly than those of many younger men could have done.

The boy Jake had "turned up" directly after the departure of the rebels, with his face covered with corn meal, to the great astonishment and indignation of old Pharaoh, who "Declar'd ef he didn't b'lieve that mizzable young nigger had been an' crep into one of Missis' meal bags!" But as he

had not been caught in the act, he was not molested, and went his way rejoicing. The day after the arrival of old Bill Woodworth, Brant wished the boy, for some purpose of his own, but he was not to be found. He was searched for, all over the place, but did not make his appearance during the day. Old Pharaoh was triumphant.

"Thar, now, Massa Brant," said he, "didn't I tole ye that ar young nigger wan't no 'count? Ef you'd jest luff em long o' me, I'd 'a made a useful boy outer him. It's hard trainin' that stock o' niggers, but I'd 'a tanned his hide fur him, till he'd 'a been glad to stay put some'eres." ¿

"What do you mean by 'that stock of niggers,' Pharaoh?"

"Jest them low-raised niggers, like that yere boy, Jake, raised in low families, an' with no breedin' into 'em."

"But you can have nothing to say against that boy, Pharaoh. He is free. He does not belong to me, or to any one. Woodworth took him from his master, who was a mean traitor, and confiscated him; so he belongs either to himself or to the United States."

"Then luff the 'Nited States take car on him, Massa Brant, an' not hev him a-runnin' round loose, so. A boy like him has got to b'long to somebody."

"Pharaoh, I am astonished to hear you speak so, when I know that you believe in freedom."

"Yes, Massa Brant; jest so. So I'se 'stonished at myself. Goramighty's bressed freedom is for all, to be sure, even for sech as him. Sometimes I think, an' sometimes again I don't think, that Goramighty's freedom is a great thing. But that ar little nigger, Massa Brant, needs somebody to take car o' him, an' train him up."

"Well, Pharaoh, perhaps he has gone off with Woodworth."

"P'raps he has. Thank the Lord I ain't 'sponsible for him."

In the meantime, the fortification of the smoke-house was completed, and all other preparations were made, to meet a sudden attack. Major Mercer sent to a place of safety the few negroes he had upon the farm, saving only old Pharaoh, Harvey, Pete, and two other able-bodied men, together with Aunt Jule and a girl. He provisioned the smoke-house, and conveyed to it the arms and ammunition, and such of his valuables as could be spared from the house, for which ample room was found in the cellar. Brant, Charley Mercer, and old Pharaoh, continued to scout and watch for guerillas.

CHAPTER XX.

The Siege of the Smoke-house.

DURING three days after the departure of Jake, the "outpost" was undisturbed, but on the morning of the fourth old Pharaoh was confounded, and Brant's belief was verified, by the return of the boy in hot haste, with a message from Woodworth, to the effect that they must move into the smoke-house immediately, and expect an attack. When the boy had been given something to eat and drink—for he seemed to be half famished, and nearly worn out—he repeated the story that Woodworth had told him, as nearly as he could. It appeared that the rebels had discovered that the family of Major Mercer was a Union family, and that it contained a son—Charles—who would be an excellent subject for conscription. It also seemed that old Mike Curwin, intent on revenge and blood money, had been spying around, and had learned, or had reason to suspect, that Brant was harbored at the house. But the most important part, a part that could only be dimly guessed at through the indistinct account of the boy, was that Brant's character had become fully known, as well as his connection with Major Mercer, and an order had been sent from Jackson for the arrest of his guest, dead or alive. Consequently a strong guerilla party had set out from camp for that purpose.

On receiving this intelligence, it was the work of but a few moments to move into the smoke-house, and all due preparations were made in a very short time.

"Major Mercer," said Brant, when they were in the building, "I feel that I have brought this upon you—in fact, I know that I have—and I am sorry to have been the cause of much suffering and loss to you."

"Not a bit of it, sir. Not a bit of it. If you have been, in any manner, the cause of what has happened to me, you deserve my everlasting esteem, and I thank you for it. I never felt better in my life than I do now—never felt half so free or so happy. If they fight us, as I suppose they will, I am confident that we will beat them, as sure of it as I am standing here."

"I hope so, sir, and will do my best to make your words good."

"I stand corrected, my boy. You young ones are always teaching me something, against my will. Let us not be too confident, but put our trust in God and our good cause, and keep our powder dry. Now, let us look to our arms and ammunition."

The arms were distributed as follows: The Major had his German rifle, and Brant and Charley were armed with those which Woodworth had brought. To old Pharaoh was given a common country rifle, and to Harvey another. Both were skilled in the use of this weapon. Pete had the shot-gun, well loaded with buck-shot and ball, but was instructed not to use it except at easy range. The boy, Jake, and the other two black men, were to assist as they could. Mrs. Mercer and Mabel, Aunt Jule and the girl, were in readiness to descend into the cellar if an attack should commence. The building was lighted partly by the ventilation holes under the roof, and partly by lanterns.

Thus all things were in readiness, and watches were set upon the road, and the little party waited patiently for an attack. But noon came, and no enemy, and all except the watchers ate heartily of a good cold dinner. The appetite of Major Mercer was excellent, and he was in fine spirits.

But they were not allowed to remain much longer in suspense. Harvey and little Jake shortly came in, and brought the news that a body of horsemen was coming up the road, with a flag flying. The doors were closed and barred, and the women were sent below, while the men took their stations.

The horsemen soon came in sight, a loose and straggling crowd of men, riding with scarcely any attempt at order or discipline. They appeared to number a hundred, or more. In the front were a few files of regular rebel cavalry, but the rest were unmitigated guerillas, of the worst stamp, with scarcely any attempt at uniform, and with all sorts of arms. They were halted in front of the house, which stood at a little distance from the road, and three men, dismounting, went up and knocked at the door. Receiving no reply, they shouted back to their officer:

"They won't answer, Captain."

"Then burst in the door."

That was quickly done, and the men disappeared within the house. In about ten minutes they came out, and again shouted:

"No one here, Captain. The birds have flown.

"They can't have flown far. They must be about here somewhere."

"My God!" exclaimed Major Mercer, "that officer is the man who kicked me. I'll shoot him while I can."

"No, father," said Charley, seizing the Major's arm as he grasped his rifle, "we should not draw them upon us unnecessarily."

"Don't touch me, boy; I will."

The Major put his rifle out of the loophole, and fired hastily. He had not taken proper aim, but the officer's horse was seen to stagger, and then fall. The rider, however, rose, and pointed toward the smoke house with his sword. He then withdrew his men a short distance, and appeared to hold a consultation with some of them.

Shortly one of the number issued from their disorderly ranks, mounted, and carrying a white handkerchief or rag upon a stick. Major Mercer mounted upon a box, and put his head through a trap in the roof, which had been arranged for the purpose of reconnoitering. When the rebels had approached within speaking distance, he hailed him:

"Don't come any nearer! Who are you, and what do you want?"

The man halted his horse, and answered:

"I come from Captain Woolson, of the Kentucky Rangers, to demand the surrender of Major Henry Mercer, his son, Charles, and a Yankee spy, name unknown, and satisfaction for firing on the flag of the Confederacy."

"Tell Captain Woolson, if he is a Captain, that I, Henry Mercer, refuse to acknowledge his authority, or that of any traitor. Tell him, also, that I fired upon him, and struck his horse, and will be pleased to have him come a little nearer, so that I can manage to put a ball through him."

"Captain Woolson also instructed me to say that if you do not surrender immediately, he will burn down your house, and then smoke you out of this den."

"Let him burn! He will suffer for it."

The Major then let down the trap, and the man returned to his comrades.

The rebels were seen to divide, and shortly advanced against the building upon three sides. As they came, Charley Mercer quickly ran up, through an aperture in the roof, near which a light pole was fastened, the beautiful Union flag which his mother and sister had made. They could not see it floating from the pole, but knew, by the yells of the rebels, that it was plainly visible. Then arose from the smoke-house the sound of the manly voices of Brant and Charley Mercer, singing:

"'Tis the star-spangled banner, oh, long may it wave,
O'er the land of the *free* and the *home* of the brave."

The answer was a yell of rage, and a volley of musket and rifle balls, that rattled harmlessly against the stout sides of the building. The reply from the smoke-house was as speedy, and far more effective. The Major, with his cartridges, and Brant and Charley with their breech-loading rifles, loaded and fired rapidly, but with careful aim; while old Pharaoh and Harvey rammed down their bullets, and worked with a will that showed they were deserving of life, if not of freedom.

The dismounted rebels soon sought what cover they could, but continued their fire, showing a contempt of danger that would have been admirable in a better cause. Three of their bullets had entered the loopholes, but no harm had been done, except the clipping off of a piece of old Pharaoh's ear. The main body, however, soon withdrew out of range, and then the flames were seen to issue from the house. As the smoke and fire ascended, the Major jumped up and down in an ecstacy.

"Let it burn!" he cried, "let it burn! I am glad of it. They have paid for it already, if their miserable lives are worth any thing."

While the house was burning, there was a temporary lull in the attack, interrupted only by a few dropping shots from the rebel marksmen. As Charley Mercer was peering through a loophole, he perceived a man crawling over the ground near them, and occasionally leaping on under cover of the smoke.

"There is a skulking scoundrel," said he. "I will soon fix his flint for him."

"No, Massa Charles; don't shoot!" cried Jake, who was also on the lookout. "It's Massa Bill! it's Massa Bill!"

The crawler suddenly bounded up, and

sprung toward the building. He was instantly discovered by the rebels, and several voices cried:

"It's old Woodworth! Shoot him down."

They then appeared from their places of concealment, and twenty bullets whistled around the old scout, but he was unharmed, while the guerillas paid dearly for their temerity. Brant and Charley speedily opened the door for him, and barred it behind him.

"Hope ye're all alive and safe," said the old man, as he entered. "I was kinder 'feared I couldn't git to ye 'thout losin' old Bess,"—showing his long rifle—but I brought her safe through. Ye can't tell what a splendid guide that flag o' yourn was to me, through the smoke!"

The old man was heartily welcomed, and consented to eat something, his voracity showing that he needed refreshment. Major Mercer then served out rations of brandy, and the defenders of the fort rested from their labors, with the exception of watchers at the loopholes at each angle, who occasionally took a shot at the skulking guerilla.

"Ye've fit 'em off right well, Major," said Woodworth, "an' I reckon ye ken keep on doin' it, as ye're well fixed. I don't think they'll be apt to trouble us agin afore night."

"I am of the same opinion," said Brant. "I think they are preparing for a night attack. I wish we had some hand-grenades."

"The best thing ye ken do is to git all the rest ye ken, till they come on agin. One o' these yere niggers an' I ken keep good enough watch onto 'em."

The garrison then made themselves as easy and comfortable as circumstances would permit; and the day wore away into the night, without any special molestation. The night was cloudy and dark, and Woodworth at last told them that they had better hold themselves in readiness for any emergency.

"Hev yer pistols ready," said he, "an' knives ef ye've got 'em, fur it may come to close work. Hark! I hear somethin', but can't see nothin'."

The words were hardly out of his mouth, when there was a great crash against the door, and it was nearly burst from its hinges. The little garrison was taken by surprise, but had their wits about them when the next crash came, and the door fell. Brant sprung at the opening, pistol in hand, but his foot slipped, and he had nearly fallen. A stalwart guerilla raised a huge bowie-knife, and that moment would have been the last of Bob Brant's life, had not the

boy Jake suddenly leaped up before him, and the heavy knife sunk into the black boy's brain with a dull, sickening crash. The next instant the rifle of old Bill sung death to the guerilla; and then the negro Pete proved himself the man for the emergency, by discharging both barrels of his shot-gun into the crowd that was pressing into the doorway. The effect was terrible, resembling that of a charge of canister, and driving them back with shrieks and yells. Old Bill sprung through the doorway, with brandished knife, followed by the rest, and a fierce hand-to-hand fight ensued, in which the rebels, who had not yet recovered from the dose given them by Pete, became panic stricken, and fled in dismay. The victorious garrison then hastily reëntered the building, carrying in their dead and wounded. The dead proved to be Harvey and the boy Jake. Pete was severely wounded, and the rest had not escaped. Charley Mercer had an ugly gash on his arm, and Brant had been momentarily stunned by a blow on the head. The body of Harvey was then placed within the small addition, and the door was more securely barricaded. When Jake was examined, he was found to be still alive, but was senseless, and soon breathed his last.

"Thar, now," said old Bill, "lies a little nigger as I must confess I was disapp'inted into. I didn't reckon he'd got so much grit. He's free now, poor feller, but it's sartin he arnt his freedom in this life, though he didn't git to see much of it."

Brant bent over the black face, and tears came in his eyes.

"He died to save my life, and he did save it. Do you think he needed taking care of, Pharaoh? He has gone now where he will be well taken of forever."

"Now, Massa Brant, donty say that! Donty say it jest now. I wish I hadn't never said nothin' agin that poor boy, but I was kinder sot agin that stock o' niggers."

"We're well outer that scrape" said old Bill, "But 'twas hot work. They'll be keerful not to come near us agin to-night, arter that scrimmage. Let's take a drop o' suthin' all round, an' be ready fur 'em in the mornin'."

The fort was then "put to rights," though not in the female sense of the phrase, and the ladies, with Aunt Jule and the girl, were invited up to breathe such air as the inside of the house afforded.

Charley Mercer's arm was bound up and

placed in a sling, but he laughed at the hurt, and said that he would show them in the morning, if he had a chance, that he could use his rifle yet.

CHAPTER XXI.

The Siege Raised.

As Woodworth had predicted, the garrison was not again disturbed during the night. At the first dawn of day, all eyes were strained to obtain a view of the enemy. Charley Mercer at first exclaimed that they had all gone, but he was soon undeceived by the old scout, whose practiced eye perceived men still lurking around, and he knew that the main body could not be far off. They had taken advantage of the night to carry off their dead and wounded, so that those in the smoke-house had no means of ascertaining the amount of damage they had inflicted.

"Thar's some deviltry goin' on now, 'mong them chaps," said Woodworth, after a careful survey of the situation, an' it won't be long afore they let us know what they're up to, neither."

He was right, for they had hardly had time to eat a hasty breakfast, when the rebels were again seen defiling up the road. They had evidently been reinforced, for more men in uniform were among them, and this time, to the dismay of the party in the smoke-house, they brought a small brass cannon on wheels.

"I'm 'feared it's all up with us now, Mr. Brant," said the old scout, with a sigh, "ef that thing 'll shoot any ways far; but we ken jest die like men."

"I am not so sure of that," answered Bob. "That gun does not seem to be more than a four-pounder, and they can hardly hurt us much without shell, which they are not likely to have. We can give them trouble yet."

"That's true, sir, but a four-pound ball mought smash even these yere logs, and I've hearn that splinters are awful things."

The rebels soon placed their gun in position in the road, and the marksmen scattered around the building and commenced to fire at the loopholes.

"Now, Mr. Brant," said the old scout, "do you an' old Pharaoh 'tend to them chaps 'round the house as well as ye ken,

an' the Major an' I'll jest bother that pop-gun a bit. Major, you mark that man with the rammer, an' I'll take him with the fire."

The Major took a long aim, and as the rebel with the rammer stood in front of the gun, he fired, and the man fell. Another seized the rammer, but another shot was heard, and the other dropped the rammer and limped off. The last shot came from Charley Mercer, who had thrown aside his sling, and proved that he could use his rifle yet. Another man approached the gun with the rammer, and the Major fired again, but missed, and the shot was rammed home. As the man with the match stepped up, old Bill's rifle cracked, and he fell in his tracks.

"Ef I don't mistake," said the scout, "that feller with the fire was old Mike Curwin. Ef so it be, thar's one cussed sinner gone to his account, an' a hard account 'twill be fur him, I reckon."

The rebels hastily withdrew their piece, and fired, but the shot fell short, eliciting a laugh of derision from the garrison, who now directed their attention to the scattered marksmen.

But those in charge of the artillery were not to be foiled so easily. They soon found a partial cover for the gun, much nearer the smoke-house than the place of their first attempt.

"We've got to ketch it now," said old Bill, as he sighted his long rifle, ready to drop the first man who showed himself.

Two men fell under the close aim of the scout and Major Mercer, before the piece was loaded; but when it was fired, the party saw cause to despair. It struck the building with a force that made it tremble, and passed through the wall. It was a spent shot when it entered, but a splinter struck the Major on the head and laid him senseless. There was no time to think of him then, for their foes were pressing them on all sides, and another ball from the gun passed clear through the logs, scattering the splinters fearfully. For a few moments the fire of the gun ceased, as some person of importance appeared to have fallen before Woodworth's unerring rifle.

"Mr. Mercer," said the old man, "you may as well look to yer father. We'll do what we ken, but that thar cussed gun is killin' us."

"As we can not go out and take it," said Bob, with a mournful smile, "we will have to stay in here and take it."

"Hark!" exclaimed the scout, eagerly

placing his ear to the ground. "I hear a tramplin', like horses. Yes! it's horses, sure as yer born, an' plenty of 'em too."

"More rebels, perhaps."

"I don't believe it. They ain't apt to ride that reg'lar."

"Is it Blucher or Grouchy? We will soon see." As Bob spoke, he fired at a rebel who was loading the gun, and more by good luck than aim, brought him down.

Just then there came a roaring cheer down the road, followed by a rattling volley, and the rebels left their gun, threw down their arms, and stampeded in all directions, as a squadron of Union cavalry came in sight. The cavalrymen scattered after them, cutting them down and capturing them right and left.

"Did you know Fort Henry was taken, you rebel wretches?" shouted a Union officer as he galloped after the retreating guerillas.

The door of the smoke-house was thrown open; the women were brought up from the cellar, and the remainder of the garrison emerged and greeted their deliverers. Major Mercer was brought out into the open air, where he soon revived, but there was an ugly wound in his head.

Woodworth was recognized by the officer in command of the squadron, who informed him that Fort Henry had fallen, and the victorious army of Grant and the victorious gunboats of Foote were on their way to Donelson. The news seemed too good to be true. The officer said that he was on a reconnoitering expedition, when he was attracted to the spot by the firing of the cannon. Thus, that which seemed about to prove their ruin, had in reality proved their salvation.

It only remained to gather up the fragments, and seek a place of safety. The bodies of Harvey and the boy Jake were buried near where they fell, and the graves were properly marked. The wounded Major and Pete were placed in litters and carried by a detail of the soldiers to the residence of Mrs. Mercer's brother, where the rest of the family followed them.

Bob Brant accompanied them to the house, but did not remain, as he considered it his duty now, more than ever, to be with the army. Accordingly he bid them farewell, and made a second visit to Donelson. In the bloody battle which ensued, he distinguished himself, and rendered efficient services, as a volunteer aid. He entered the fort in triumph this time, but with the loss of his left arm, which was taken off by a shell. It was more than a month before he could go to Mabel, to be nursed again, but when he did, he was happy to find that her love was not at all diminished, but rather increased, by the loss of his arm. In due time, with the glad concurrence of all parties, they were married, and have not as yet seen any reason whatever to secede from that Union.

Major Mercer recovered a large portion of his property, upon the Federal occupation of Jackson. Charley Mercer entered the Union army, and, of course, distinguished himself.

Old Bill Woodworth lived to serve his country to some purpose. With that purity and earnestness of nature which distinguish the true patriot, he labored, in his humble but important position, steadily and nobly. Let us hope to make our readers better acquainted with him and his achievements.

THE END.

www.ingramcontent.com/pod-product-compliance
Lightning Source LLC
Chambersburg PA
CBHW022202020726
47496CB00008B/2846